A SECRET WORD

A NOVEL

JENNIFER PADDOCK

A TOUCHSTONE BOOK
Published by Simon & Schuster
New York   London   Toronto   Sydney

TOUCHSTONE
Rockefeller Center
1230 Avenue of the Americas
New York, NY 10020

Portions of this novel first appeared elsewhere, in slightly different form: "The
Ones Who Are Holding Things Up" in *The South Carolina Review,* "Talk Like
Friends" in *Louisiana Literature,* "A Matter of Someone Leaving" in *The North American Review,* "And When I Should Feel Something" in *Stories from the Blue Moon Café,*
and "Intimate and Dark" in *Other Voices.*

"Responsible" by Freedy Johnston © 1994 Warner-Tamerlane Publishing Corp.,
Brazen Red Music & Trouble Tree Music. All rights administered by Warner-
Tamerlane Publishing Corp. All rights reserved. Used by permission. Warner Bros.
Publications U.S. Inc., Miami, FL 33014.
"Late Fragment" from *A New Path to the Waterfall* by Raymond Carver. Copyright
©1989 by estate of Raymond Carver. Used by permission of Grove/Atlantic, Inc.

For information regarding special discounts for bulk purchases,
please contact Simon & Schuster Special Sales at
1-800-456-6798 or business@simonandschuster.com

Designed by Michelle Blau

Manufactured in the United States of America

10 9 8 7 6 5 4 3 2 1

Library of Congress Cataloging-in-Publication Data
   Paddock, Jennifer.
      A secret word : a novel / Jennifer Paddock.
         p. cm.
      "A Touchstone book."
      I. Title.
   PS3616.A3355S43 2004
   813'.6—dc22   2003057343

ISBN 0-7432-4707-8

To my husband, Sidney Thompson;
my mother, Anita Paddock;
and to the memory of my father, Ben L. Paddock.

CONTENTS

But I want somebody to lie
And to lock me out of the years
And I want my problem again
And a secret word you will not hear
—Freedy Johnston, "Responsible"

But she seemed to know, too, when to stop listening to
it, as if all of what little or much wisdom there
is in the world were suddenly hers.
—J. D. Salinger, *Franny and Zooey*

A Secret
Word

THE ONES WHO ARE HOLDING THINGS UP

November 1986

Chandler

Leigh is the kind of girl who hangs around girls who get in fights. Not that she wears rock-concert T-shirts, but she does smoke. She and I are different, but we are friends. She's been to my house, three stories with woods and a lake in back, a game room, halls you can do cartwheels down. And I've been to her house, dark and small and sad.

Sarah is beautiful and theatrical and is my best friend and has been since the day I almost killed her. When we were eight, she talked the assistant golf pro into letting us hit range balls, and she walked right behind me on my backswing. There was screaming and blood and an ambulance, and seventeen stitches to the back of her head in the shape of a *C,* my own initial. Then we began taking tennis lessons and now are known as *those tennis girls.* A tournament can get us out of school for a week. We go to a public school and make good grades without studying. We are on the outside of the inner circle of cool kids but are cool enough.

I'm in Spanish class zoning out, not listening to the scratchy record of a Mexican family having a conversation at breakfast. I'm thinking about my plan for lunch today with Leigh and Sarah, maybe at the country club, and wondering how that would go.

My father tells me that where we live, in Fort Smith, Arkansas, used to be called "Hell on the Border." It was a place people passed through: Cherokee Indians on the Trail of Tears, gold miners to California, trappers canoeing upriver, ranchers headed to Texas, outlaws seeking freedom.

I imagine there are worse places to grow up, and I am lucky to be rich and to love my parents, but I do not love it here. I will pass through.

Between first and second period, at my locker, I see Leigh at her locker, tapping a pack of Camel Lights, and when she catches my eye, I start to walk over, but somebody, a real genius of slapstick, comes up behind me and pushes the back side of my right knee, causing my leg to buckle, and I almost trip. I turn around with a little agitation and find Sarah smiling her coy Sarah smile.

"Falling apart at the seams, Chandler?" she says. Then Trey, the running back, rushes Sarah, taking her in a headlock, holding her like he's in love, and I wonder if Sarah notices this, and when he lets go, there is purple dye smeared across his white jersey. Sarah is always dying her hair. She probably just did it thirty minutes ago, staying home during first period, using one of the drawerful of late notes her mom has written for her.

I watch Trey pushing Sarah down the hall.

"Trey's walking me to class," Sarah yells back. "I'll meet you on the court."

Second period Sarah and I have gym, and so does Leigh, but Coach McGavin lets Sarah and me play tennis, while Leigh and all the other girls have to square dance with the PE boys. I look around for Leigh. I know she has a car today because I saw her pulling into the lot in her mom's old Chrysler, a two-tone two-door.

Sarah and I aren't sixteen yet like Leigh is, even though we're all in the tenth grade, so every day we try to find an older kid with a car to take us off campus for lunch. We've never asked

Leigh to take us because you never know when she's going to have her mother's car. Mostly we ask this sweet guy who's a senior in the band, a trombone player, and sometimes we go with this swimmer girl who's a junior with a Bronco. If we ask guys, we always ask guys we would never want to go out with. It would be too humiliating to beg for a ride from a senior on the football team like Trey. But I don't see Leigh anywhere.

I'm late to gym, but I don't mind. I actually prefer it because I hate undressing in front of the other girls. It's not that I'm overweight or ugly or anything. Though I'm cute enough and have blonde hair, I'm shorter and look younger than the others, with smaller hips and breasts. At home, everyone is always covered up. My mother wears a pink or blue cotton nightgown and a pink flowery robe, and my father wears neat Brooks Brothers pajamas with a tattered terry-cloth robe that used to be brick red, but is now pale with spots from too much washing.

Sarah likes undressing in front of other people. When I spend the night at her house, she'll walk down the hall from the bathroom to the bedroom, naked and thin, her straight past-the-shoulders hair hidden under a towel knotted in front, and when I stand there frozen, watching, Sarah says, "What?"

I see Sarah already on the court, sweatpants on, her lucky blue Fila jacket tied around her waist. She's hitting her serve so hard that it bounces in the square, then flies to the metal fence with a clang. My serve takes a couple bounces before it hits the fence with barely a rattle. I can still beat Sarah, though I know it's only a matter of time until she learns to play more consistently, eases up on her power, mixes up her shots. Right now it's a head game—our matches are close, but I always win.

When I was nine, I went the entire summer, at least ten tournaments in all parts of Arkansas, beating my opponents, even Sarah, 6–0, 6–0. I'm so dreamy about the days when I used to kill everyone.

Sarah and I play a groundstroke game to eleven. I win, barely, by hitting the same shot, deep with topspin, every time. I really do get into a kind of rhythm, and I start thinking of myself like a Buddhist monk chanting *one two three hit* or like my father who meditates saying the same secret word over and over.

Afterward, we fill up an empty tennis-ball can with water and take turns drinking and talk about what we're going to do for lunch.

"We could stay here," I kid. "Get a Coke and an ice-cream sandwich and stand outside."

"Ah, Chandler baby, no," Sarah says, and I smile.

We start walking back to get dressed for third period, and I spot Leigh smoking under the stadium bleachers. She's long-limbed and awkward there in the shadows but has a pretty face, her wavy brown hair pulled back by two silver barrettes.

I twirl my racquet twice and catch it on the grip. "Why aren't you inside square dancing?" I ask.

"They don't ever miss me," Leigh says.

"Can I have one of those?" Sarah says, then sets her racquet and the tennis balls on the ground.

"Sure," Leigh says, like she's honored that Sarah would smoke one of her cigarettes, and lights it for her. Sarah and Leigh don't really know each other, only a little about each other through me.

"Hey, Leigh," I say, thinking about my lunch plan, and I take the rubber band out of my hair, letting my ponytail fall. "Did your mom call in sick?"

Leigh doesn't answer, just gives me a look like she's ashamed.

"I don't mean anything by it," I say. "I just wondered if you have the car today?"

"I have the car."

"You're sixteen?" Sarah says.

"Yeah, since October." Leigh pauses a moment, taking a drag and looking at us. "Why, do y'all want to go to lunch?"

I smile. "That'd be great. Thanks, Leigh." I reach out for a smoke, and Leigh lights my cigarette off hers, then flicks hers away.

Sarah lets her hand fall to the side and drops her half-smoked cigarette in the grass. "So, how about Hardscrabble?"

Hardscrabble is the name of the country club where Sarah and I have spent nearly every day of our lives playing tennis. I used to think the name was a golfing term, but my dad told me it's because the golf course used to be a farm, which was known, because of its rocky conditions, as a "hardscrabble" way to make a living. It seems weird to me that it's a name of a place where rich people go to take it easy.

"Definitely," I say. "Hardscrabble."

"Do we have time?" says Leigh.

"I have study hall next period," I say. "I can call in our order. No problem."

"But I'm not a member," Leigh says.

"We know, and we'll buy," Sarah says. "What do you want?"

Leigh gathers her hair in her hand, then lets it go. "Maybe a turkey sandwich. With bacon."

"You mean a *club sandwich?*" Sarah says.

"I guess," says Leigh.

"All right, Leigh," I say. "We'll meet you in the parking lot right when the bell rings. We have to beat everyone out and get there, or we'll never finish in time. It's like a sit-down dinner."

"I know," Leigh says. "We'll get there fast. I'm a good driver."

"Then we'll see you later," Sarah says. She picks up her racquet and the can of balls and walks away, and with the cigarette in one hand and my racquet in the other, I follow.

In study hall, all the football players sit in the back and never study. The closest they come to any real work is copying assignments from me or any other humanitarian who will let them. Trey is always goofing off and thinks it's funny to hold up notes written in big letters that say something like, "Hi, Chandler." I always smile when he does that, even though I know it's subnormal.

Trey and I went to the movies once, and he called my house right before he was supposed to show up and asked my dad, who rarely answers the phone, to ask me if I would iron his shirt for him. My dad was laughing and yelled the message up to my room, and I yelled back that I would. And when Trey came to the door, my dad actually answered because he said he wanted to meet *this* boy. Usually, if I had a date, my dad would run and hide in the kitchen and leave my mother or me to open the door. It's not that my dad doesn't care about who I go out with. He just doesn't know what to say. And neither did Trey and I on our one and only date.

Coach McGavin runs the study hall. What an easy schedule he has—gym and study hall. I walk up to him, and he gives me the pass before I even say what I want it for. "Thanks, Coach," I say. I go to the pay phone and call Hardscrabble's clubhouse, where we like to eat lunch. They also have a snack bar, but it's not nearly as nice as the clubhouse. I order a club sandwich for Leigh and two French dips for Sarah and me. I tell the guy who answers to have it ready at 11:30, that we're coming from school, that we only have forty minutes. He says, "No problem. Last name Carey, right?" I feel a little embarrassed that he knows my voice. I say politely as I can, "That's right. Thanks so much."

Sarah and I meet by the trophy case and walk out to the parking lot together. Leigh is already waiting for us in her mom's car.

"Cool," I say, getting into the backseat.

"Yeah, Leigh," Sarah says and shuts the door. "How'd you get out here so fast?"

"I left physics early."

"You must have Mr. Holbrook," Sarah says. "I have him first period, and I'm always late. He doesn't care."

"Well, we can't be late coming back from lunch," I tell Leigh. "We have geometry fourth. Mrs. Schneider."

Leigh nods and starts driving. "Want some music?"

"Yeah, baby," Sarah says and starts turning the dial.

We're just about to leave the lot when we hear a horn blaring behind us. We all turn to see Trey hanging halfway out the window of his new black Firebird, his white jersey waving. We take a right and a quick left onto Cliff Drive, the road that Hardscrabble Country Club is on, and Trey follows us, with his shiny chrome rims, his big tires, his tail fin high in the air.

"God, what a tacky car," I say.

"It's not that bad," Sarah says. "I kind of like it."

"I'd rather be in this one," I say. "Right, Leigh?"

Leigh turns back and smiles at me, then looks ahead, speeding up a little. Cliff Drive is a long, windy road lined with expensive houses with long driveways. It's hard to see the houses from the road, but Leigh keeps glancing back and forth, trying to see something. Sarah rolls down her window and climbs halfway out, the purple streaks in her dark hair blowing, and yells "woo" over to Trey like she's at a concert.

"Good Lord," I say and pull on her to get back in. "Be careful."

"Hey," she says. "Relax."

As we round the corner coming up to the club, I turn around and see Trey taking the curve too fast. His car swings off the road, jackknifes, then goes into a ditch, only his stupid tail fin showing. Sarah sees it, too, and laughs.

"What a moron!" I say.

"What is it?" asks Leigh, and Sarah tells her what she missed.

Leigh slows down and takes the exit for Hardscrabble. She circles the lot, hesitating. "Should we go back?"

"No, he's fine," I say. "He's wrecked there twice before."

"Yeah, don't worry about little Trey, Leigh baby," Sarah says. "Try to park up front."

"Yeah," I say. "Time is of the essence." This is a phrase my mother uses when I'm running late, which is almost always.

We rush into the country club and walk through the bar, and Sarah and I grab nuts and mints from little bowls set around on small marble tables. In the dining room, we sit by a window, so we have a good view of the golf course. Sarah tells Leigh about how I almost killed her with a 7 iron. She always tells that story whenever she gets the chance.

A waiter comes up to us with menus, but I tell him we already ordered by phone, and he smiles and fills our water glasses and takes our drink order. I get a Coke like always, and Sarah gets a virgin strawberry daiquiri, and Leigh orders iced tea.

Leigh leans over and says in a hushed voice, "Is everyone that works here black?"

I shrug. "I guess."

"I think I've seen a few white ones before," Sarah says, then waves her hand and gets a different waiter to bring us crackers and bread and butter.

"This is really nice," Leigh says. "Thanks for bringing me here."

"Thanks for driving us here," Sarah says, buttering a cracker.

The waiter returns with our sandwiches on a big round tray he carries with one hand above his shoulder, and another waiter follows him, like he's the other waiter's waiter, carrying our drinks.

"Cool," I say. "We still have twenty-seven minutes."

On the side of Leigh's plate are silver cups with mayonnaise and mustard, and she spreads both on each layer of the four triangles of her sandwich. Sarah and I dig into our French dips and have a silver cup of ketchup between us for our fries.

"This is way better than the school cafeteria," Leigh says.

"Chandler and I," says Sarah, "have never eaten there. We've successfully gotten a ride every day for three months. And in just four more months, we won't have to. I'm sixteen in March."

"When are you sixteen, Chandler?" Leigh says.

I take a drink of my Coke. "Not until next September."

"God," Leigh says. "I'm almost a year older."

"Chandler's got a bad birthday," Sarah explains, holding her virgin daiquiri like it's real. "If she were just one month younger, she could play sixteen-and-under tennis for an extra year." Sarah waves her drink around. "So Leigh, what's up with your mom?"

Leigh takes a bite of her sandwich, then a drink of her iced tea. "What do you mean?"

I eat a fry and Leigh doesn't say anything, so I say, "Nothing's up with her. She just calls in sick a lot."

"She hates working," Leigh says.

"Man, I don't blame her." Sarah raises her glass and says, "To not ever having to work."

Leigh smiles, and I smile.

"Let's get out of here," I say. "Time is of the essence."

I raise my hand for the waiter, and he brings over our ticket, and I sign my father's name with a short yellow pencil, *Ben L. Carey #379.*

We have about five minutes before the bell rings. What takes the most time is finding a parking place in the school lot. But Leigh tells us not to worry about it and that if we're late getting back, she'll drop us off by the door.

Leigh turns on the radio and switches the dial around and stops on a commercial that we all know by heart, and we say together in a deep, dopey voice, "C&H Tire. 8701 Rogers. Where we do it just for you."

Leigh takes a right onto Cliff Drive, and we only go about ten yards because there's so much traffic. It normally gets a little backed up every day with kids rushing from McDonald's or Wendy's, but this is way worse than usual.

Sarah's in the backseat this time, and she yells up, "What the hell?"

Leigh is quiet, concentrating, moving the car slowly.

"I can't tell," I say. I roll down the window and lean out as far as I can. In the distance, I can see a fire truck and blue police lights. A cop is waving cars around.

Sarah leans up, too, and tries to get a look. "Is that all for Trey?" she says.

"It has to be," Leigh says.

We creep forward, and as we approach the curve, I see Trey's black Firebird still tipped down into the ditch. His shiny chrome rims, his big tires, his tail fin.

"That looks pretty bad," Leigh says.

I feel relieved when I see Trey standing there by a cop. He looks fine. The back of his white jersey is clean around the number and not torn or anything. The cop is probably talking to him about the big away game tonight in Pine Bluff, which is pretty far from Fort Smith, about four hours. I think the football team is supposed to leave right after lunch. Trey's probably worried about missing the bus. "Thank God," I say. "He's okay. He's right there."

Sarah is still leaning up over the seat, but she doesn't say anything.

"That's not him," Leigh says. "That's someone else. Trey's #68."

"She's right," Sarah says.

Leigh inches the car forward, then the policeman directing traffic makes us stop, and we're right next to Trey's car. Leigh shifts into park, and we all look. The front end is crumpled by at least three feet against the side of the ditch. Firemen are working to cut Trey out. The door is open, but his body is wrapped around the steering wheel. His head stuffed between the dash and the windshield. There is blood on his jersey and on his head and in the cracks of the glass.

I look away and notice that people are starting to drive around us and that we're the ones who are holding things up. The policeman knocks on the back of our car and startles us, tells us to get moving. Leigh puts the car in drive, and we proceed.

Nobody says anything. Maybe we don't know what to say, or what to think. I look at one of the fancy houses and think that I like my house better. And I like Sarah's house even better than mine. She lives in this long sprawling one on the other side of Hardscrabble, on the back nine of the golf course. Sometimes, when I spend the night over there, we'll sneak out and meet guys.

One night Trey met us there with another football player. I was the one who was supposed to be with Trey, but we still had the same problem talking to each other. We lay down on a green, the short grass more perfect than carpet, and looked at the stars. We never kissed, but he put his arm around me, and his other hand rubbed on my shoulder and on my elbow and on my wrist and on my palm and on each finger. He was the first boy to ever touch me like that, and I never even kissed him.

Traffic is moving almost back to normal. The second lunch has already started, and we see kids breeze by the other way, not knowing what's ahead.

Leigh turns off the radio. Sarah starts crying. Leigh looks over to me, and I look back to her, then put my hand over my eyes. Sarah's breathing is loud and erratic. Leigh turns into the lot.

"You can go ahead and park," I say.

"No, I'll drop you off," she says. "I want to."

She pulls up to the entrance of the school, and I wipe my eyes.

"You sure?" I ask. "We'll wait and walk in with you."

"No, go ahead," she says.

I open my door and get out, then pull the seat forward for Sarah. I grip her arm and steady her until she's standing. I start to thank Leigh for the ride but stop myself. I want to tell her that I'm sorry, that we should've gone back, I should've let her go back, but I don't say anything, just shut the door and watch her drive off, all by herself, looking for a place to park.

Sarah and I walk into the school, and I'm wondering how long it will take to forget this walk. It seems too quiet. There should be a commotion in the halls. Others saw what we saw, but classes have already started, and we are going to be late.

Talk Like Friends

Leigh

I work at the counter of Sunny Day Cleaners. It's not really that bad a job. I don't have to steam, press, or even sack the clothes. The worst part is my hours—seven to seven, five days a week. The manager thinks I'm low class, or maybe he has seen me stare at his glass eye, which is bluer than the other, waiting for it to stray. He doesn't like me much, but he knows not many people would work that long, and even he'd admit my appearance is very neat, which it is on account of the three items I get to have cleaned for free each day.

And every day is the same. I talk to the customers the same way. "Hi, Mr. Smith," I say. "How are you? Do you want those pants dry cleaned or laundered? Will Friday after five-thirty be all right? See you then." Then Mr. Smith usually winks at me like most of the men who come in here do.

It's a nice change when Mrs. Carey walks in. I'm surprised to see her because normally her husband brings in their clothes. He always gives me a nod like he recognizes me, but he never says anything. *She* will. Right in front of the manager, she says, "Leigh Ingram? Oh, Leigh Ingram. I thought that was you. Aren't you pretty?"

I smile and feel a blush fall across my cheeks. "Hi, Mrs. Carey."

Mrs. Carey lays her clothes on the counter, and they look like the usual—Brooks Brothers shirts and Liz Claiborne skirts and blouses.

"How long have you been working here?" she says. She brushes her short blonde hair behind her ears, and she reminds me of her daughter, Chandler, who I was friends with in junior high and high school and who goes to college at Sewanee.

"About a month," I say. "I'm still kind of new. How's Chandler?"

She tells me Chandler's home for summer vacation, and she's driving her crazy and keeps saying she'll get a job.

I tell her we need someone here at the counter because it gets so busy in the afternoons. I say, "She wouldn't even have to work Saturdays."

The manager gets right into the show on this because the Careys bring a lot of business his way. He says, "Send her down for an interview."

Mrs. Carey nods at him. "I will." The manager walks back into his office, and Mrs. Carey leans over to me and whispers, "Does he have a glass eye?"

"Korea," I say.

"Oh," she says. "I thought so."

I watch her walk to her Oldsmobile. It's a kind of tasteful champagne color, one of those short Eighty-eights, much better than my mom's new used Chrysler, which replaces her old Chrysler. Mrs. Carey hangs her clothes in the backseat. Then she turns around and comes back in. "What should Chandler wear?"

I tell her a dress, and not to worry, that he'll take one look at her and she'll be hired. Mrs. Carey smiles at that, and for a moment I wish she were my mother, and I were Chandler, and we could leave together.

• • •

14

When I get home, Mom is actually cooking dinner and not wearing sweats. She's standing in front of the stove wearing a tight black shirt tucked into jeans. She's thin like a girl and looks good in her clothes, not like a mother should look, like Chandler's mother in her wraparound flowery skirts and loose, untucked blouses.

I say, "Not fish, I hope."

She smiles. "Spaghetti."

Mom works as a waitress at Catfish Cove, and a lot of the time she brings home leftovers. The complete works—catfish, hushpuppies, lemon wedges, and little cups of tartar sauce. I like fish, but I've had my fill of it for some time now.

I go into the kitchen to take a look. She's made a meat sauce that's starting to boil in the pan. I take a spoon and try it. "That's delicious."

"Thanks," she says. "I thought we could eat at the table."

I have to admit I like this idea, so I get out some matching napkins, plates, silverware, and two wine glasses and set the table. In the ninth grade I gave a speech on setting the table, so I know what I'm doing.

"Looks good," Mom says. She heaves out a jug of wine from a brown grocery sack.

I don't understand why she can't just buy a normal-looking bottle. "God, Mom," I say.

She puts some spaghetti and bread on our plates, and we take our seats and begin.

"Chandler Carey," I tell her, "might start working at Sunny Day."

"Why would *she* work there?"

"Her mother says she's bored and needs a job." I go on about Mrs. Carey coming in and that it looks like they got a new car.

"Must be nice to be rich," she says.

I realize I'm screwing up our family dinner, and why didn't I ask Mom about the lunch shift or did any nice men eat there or tell her she looks pretty or something? Anyway, Chandler's not the richest girl in Fort Smith. The richest girl is Chandler's best friend, Sarah Blair, and her uncle is a U.S. senator, but she only goes to school at the University of Arkansas, which is only about an hour away. She plays tennis there.

"The Careys aren't *that* rich," I say.

"Rich enough," she says.

•   •   •

Well, just like I thought, Chandler walks in looking just right in a beige linen dress and gets the job. The manager tells me to train her, but he says it in a respectful way, like because I am friends with someone like Chandler, then he must have been wrong about me.

I haven't seen Chandler for a year, not since high school, but things are the same, like how they were before Trey died, and that sort of bothers me. We never talked about Trey after his car wreck or talked much after that—not even at his funeral. And I never went to lunch with her at the country club or anywhere again.

I tell Chandler not to worry about the cash register yet. She can learn that later and may not have to at all. I explain to her that when you get to work you empty out the drawstring bags of dirty clothes and tag them. For every day of the week there is a different color tag. For clothes that will be ready on Thursday you use yellow, Friday is blue, and then purple, green, orange, and white. We're closed on Sunday. I tell her we never use red tags unless it's an emergency, like if some businessman has to catch an early plane and needs his suit cleaned first. I say if something like that happens, you take the clothes with the red tags to the Vietnamese in the back, and then it's their job to get them out by the right time.

I motion to Chandler to follow me, and we weave through steamers, washing machines, box fans. "God, it's hot," Chandler says.

I raise my voice over the noise, saying to the workers, "This is Chandler. She's new." They nod at her. "They're nice," I say. "They work hard."

She follows me to the front. I go on, "Clothes with regular tags we put in a cart, one for dry clean and one for laundry. Then we roll them to the back when they're full. Always tell the customers to pick up their clothes the next evening after five-thirty."

She nods. "Good service."

"I know," I say. "Those Vietnamese are fast. Glass Eye only pays them minimum wage. They make two dollars less an hour than we do."

Chandler writes down everything. She has a chart made out for the colors and the days and has all the prices listed. She learns a lot quicker than I do, and I think this is the first job she's ever had.

Men don't notice Chandler like I thought they would. Maybe she is too nice-looking, or maybe they know her family, and she is forbidden somehow. A lot of men flirt with me, but they've never asked me out to dinner or anything.

I have a kind of boyfriend, and I've been talking to Chandler about him all week. He's in a band and works in a record store, and I think he's pretty smart and that I can impress both of them with each other. I ask him to stop by Sunny Day, so they can meet. But when he walks in the door, I know things are bad. He has on leather pants and a concert T-shirt with the sleeves cut out. His hair looks greasy and stringy, not cool and long like I've always thought. He has the beginning of a pitiful mustache. He looks like the tackiest person I've ever seen.

Chandler offers her hand. "Nice to meet you," she says. "Leigh's told me all about you."

He doesn't shake her hand. I have to say, "Chandler, this is Cassidy."

Finally, he says, "Hi."

Normally he's not so quiet and I'm proud to be with him. He looks kind of like he's been smoking pot.

We all just stand there.

Then Cassidy says, "All right, cool," and turns around and walks out the door.

Chandler turns to me. "He looked tired. It's Friday, long week." She hesitates a moment. "Why don't you go to the pool with me tomorrow?"

"Yeah, thanks," I say, keeping my voice casual, but I'm thrilled and feel guilty at the same time—knowing she means the country club.

.   .   .

I wait for Chandler on my front steps, so she won't have to talk to my mother. I think I know why my mom doesn't like her or her parents. When I was in the seventh grade, Chandler and I were in the choir together. After we gave our Christmas concert, Chandler's parents offered to give me a ride home. It was about nine o'clock, not too late, but fairly late for a school night. I agreed, was happy to agree, because we had just moved into a nice duplex. I knew they thought I was poor, and I wanted them to see I wasn't that bad off. They pulled into my driveway behind my mother's car. My side of the duplex was completely dark or looked so at first. I told them my mom must be asleep or something and not to worry, but then Chandler said she'd like to see the inside, so I had to take her in with me. My mother wasn't home, but the TV and VCR were on and a tape was playing of a man and woman having sex, and you could see everything. There was a case of unopened beer on the coffee table, and since there was no smoke in the room, I knew my mother was with some man and had just gone out to get cigarettes, and they would be back. Chandler said to leave a note saying that I would spend the night with her. That's what I did, and my mom has been mad about it ever since.

Chandler pulls up driving her mother's Oldsmobile. I wait for her to pop the lock, then I slide in. "Can I smoke in here?" I say, taking a pack of Camel Lights from my purse.

"No, I'm sorry," Chandler says. "My mom would freak out."

"Does your mom know you smoke?"

"I don't smoke. I haven't smoked since high school," she says and backs out of the driveway.

"Yeah, I should quit myself. It *is* nice," I say, running my hand over the dash. The seats are brown leather, and there's a phone between us. "Can I call Time and Temperature?"

She grins. "Do it."

I do and it's ninety degrees with partly cloudy skies. The time is 11:07.

"I'm so white. I hope the sun stays out," Chandler says and holds her arm out the window and sails her hand in the wind.

I lift up my shirt to show her my suit. "I got a new bikini."

"Looks good," she says.

"What do you have?" I say.

"A one-piece. I'm not as daring as you."

• • •

Apparently no one at the country club is as daring as I am, and I feel pretty cheap in my two-piece. We walk to the black wrought-iron chairs near the baby pool and lay our towels over the thick orange cushions. "Time for the unveiling," Chandler says and takes off her shorts and T-shirt. Her suit is dark green with a low-cut back. I've seen it at Dillard's. Oscar de la Renta. Mine is bright yellow and purple. I got it in the teen section.

Chandler takes out Hawaiian Tropic from her bag and offers

it to me. I rub some on, and then she does. Then she pulls out a Redken bottle filled with lemon juice and water and sprays some on her hair. Then I spray some on mine. We both lie on our chairs. It's still a little cloudy, but I can feel the sun. "Thanks for taking me here," I say.

"Thanks for coming," she says.

She smiles, and her green eyes brighten with her green suit, like Tiffany glass I saw once in a magazine.

"I was always playing tennis before," she says, "and now I don't really play at all. Got burned out, I guess. We'll have to come again. I've never really been here for the pool. I feel bad not using it with my dad paying so much."

"Yeah," I say.

Chandler's father is a lawyer, and I have two pictures of him in my mind. One where he's in a dark suit, white shirt, and some conservative tie like he wears when he comes into Sunny Day. Another is at the junior-high football games, back when I was in the pep club with her. I used to watch him from the stands. He would be dressed in tan pants and a plaid shirt, carrying Cokes and popcorn. Chandler seemed so proud of him. He would walk past and give us a nod. He was the most handsome of all the fathers.

Chandler has never asked me about my father, and I've never offered the information. All I know about him is that he lives somewhere in California. He and my mother were never married.

Chandler turns her head toward me. "Do you ever think about Trey?"

I'm relieved she's finally saying something, and I sit up. "Yeah, I think about him all the time."

"You do?"

I can't believe she's surprised. Trey is the only person I've known, and I think Chandler's known, who has died. The only time I ever went to lunch with Chandler and Sarah was the day, the *moment,* he died, and we were on our way here to the country club to eat a sandwich. I was driving. I didn't see him wreck, but they did and laughed about it. He was always wrecking.

"I should have turned around," I say.

"We should have turned around," Chandler says, "but we didn't know." She lifts up and steps into her shorts. "I'll go get us a Coke."

"Could I have an iced tea? Sweetened?" I say.

"Sure," she says.

She walks away, and I quickly turn on my stomach. I adjust my suit, making sure I'm fully covered. Chandler lingers by the diving board and talks to Sarah, who is in a tennis skirt and carrying two racquets, and to some boy in golfing clothes. I see her point to me, and so I press my face into the cushion and lace my hands over my hair. I hope they're not making fun of my bikini or my new red highlights. I stay like this for a few minutes until I think it's safe.

When I do look up, the golfer is walking toward me. His skin is tan, and he has sun-bleached hair. His short-sleeved shirt and pants look lightly starched. We make eye contact.

"Hi," he says. "I'm Jonathan. A friend of Chandler's." He taps his golf shoes against the cement.

I smile. "I'm Leigh."

"I like your suit," he says.

"Yeah? Oh, I don't know."

"You look good in it."

He turns away from me and looks at the tennis courts. Sarah is hitting against the backboard. Her hair is black, but I've seen it purple and platinum. In high school, she was always changing her color. I remember Chandler playing tennis with her during gym, while everyone else had to learn to square dance on the basketball court. Sarah is a great tennis player, and Chandler used to be even better. Who wouldn't be if you lived every day of your life at the country club?

I'm thankful when Chandler shows up with my iced tea.

"So you met Leigh?" she says.

We both nod. A few moments pass. Finally, Jonathan says he has to go and meet his dad. Chandler walks him to the gate, and they talk some more.

She comes back with a big smile on her face, and I'm afraid they were laughing at me.

"How do you know him?" I say.

"From here," she says. "Our families are friends."

I grill Chandler some more and find out that he went away for high school, and now he's at Georgetown. *Georgetown*. I imagine summer dinners at the clubhouse with his parents, his mom in a sundress and his dad, like Chandler's dad, in a coat and tie. Maybe by the fall we'll be serious, and I can leave with him.

· · ·

Monday morning at Sunny Day, it's hard to concentrate. I find myself staring out the plate-glass windows to the shops across the street: Church's Fried Chicken, Peking Palace, and Jackie's Beauty Salon and Discount Fashions where Jesus is Lord and Nails are Half-Price.

When Chandler comes in, she goes straight to work, divvying up dry clean from laundry, tagging away. I feel a little guilty because she's doing work I should have already done. I start to help her. There *is* a lot to do.

On Friday there is still no mention of the country club or what Jonathan thought of me. Chandler doesn't even ask what I'm doing for the weekend. I don't ask her either. I want to. But I don't feel I have the right.

· · ·

My weekend is my own. I watch a lot of television. I order out for pizza twice. My mom isn't home. She's gone to Tulsa with a new man.

Mom has real hope for every man she meets at Catfish Cove. She knows what it's like to want more, to want to be someone else.

• • •

Monday, like all Mondays, is real busy, and Chandler and I work hard at the counter. A woman yells at me about a broken button on her husband's oxford. We're missing two skirts. The phone rings dozens of times with people asking us our hours. I can't wait for the day to be over.

At closing, Chandler tells me that something's the matter with her car, and I'm glad because I get to take her home.

Chandler tells me she likes my car. Like my mom, I bought it used, but it looks almost new. It even has a sunroof.

It's a good hot day, so I turn on the air conditioner and open the sunroof. I really want a cigarette, but I decide not to have one since Chandler doesn't smoke anymore. We are quiet most of the way to her house, then she says, "Next summer I'm not coming home. I'd like to live in New York and take a class or something."

"New York City?" I say.

"Yeah," she says. "Maybe Sarah and I could live together."

"Have you heard of the Village?"

"Greenwich Village," she says. "That's probably where I'd take my class."

I pull into Chandler's driveway. Her father is out in the front yard swinging a golf club. He gives us a wave.

"A hostess from Catfish Cove," I say, "told me that with my red highlights on my brown hair I looked like someone from the Village. She's been there before."

"Yeah," Chandler says, "you look like Sarah."

I smile.

"Maybe you could visit me."

"Oh," I say, "I'd love that."

She gets out of the car, and for a second I expect Sarah to climb out of the backseat, as if it were the day that Trey died. I want to tell her that after I dropped them off at school and was supposed to be finding a parking space, that I left the lot and went back to the wreck. I parked at the end of one of the driveways on Cliff Drive and walked through yards, faster than traffic. Trey's body was no longer pinned against the steering wheel and dash. He was on a stretcher, and a paramedic was pulling a white sheet over him, and I only caught a glimpse of his face. He looked like he had just taken off his football helmet, his hair matted down with blood instead of sweat.

But I can't say any of this because Chandler has already shut the door and is walking to her father. When she reaches him, they talk, then he hands her the golf club, and I wait and watch until she pulls back and swings.

• • •

Mom's sitting on the couch in her nightshirt watching a movie.

"What are you doing home?" I say. "I thought you had a double shift."

"I quit," she says. "I can't be a waitress anymore. I'll find something."

I look at the wood paneling, the shag carpet with stains, the tacky studio portraits, and all the little breakables that should have been broken years ago.

"Cassidy called for you," she says and holds up two fingers. "Twice."

I drop my purse to the floor. Our house is okay, I decide, and I do like Cassidy. And Mom likes him. He's always nice to her.

I get me an iced tea and sit on the couch with her. She touches my arm and rubs it a little. On many school nights, when I was in ninth grade and Trey was a junior and a starting running back and popular, he would come over to my house, and we would sit on this couch and talk like friends. He would tell me about girls he dated in high school and had sex with, and I would let him slip his hands under my clothes, but I never took them off. I liked him touching, but I didn't want him to see.

Even with Cassidy, I cover up. I tell him not to look. I turn off the lights. But unlike Trey, he doesn't beg to see. Some day, I know, I'll show him. And maybe, even if he is disappointed, he will still love me and will stay.

My mom has taken her clothes off for so many men. I've heard her, and I've gone into her room after she's been left there drunk with nothing on and dressed her. I want to tell her that she is better than a waitress, that she is better than all of the men she's taken her clothes off for. But I don't say anything. We watch the movie together. That's all.

• • •

Glass Eye is off work the rest of the week, vacationing in Destin, Florida. From the brochures he's left lying around, it looks like paradise: white beaches, aqua-green water. Chandler has a Walkman on as she methodically tags clothes, throwing them in the yellow cart. Her enthusiasm is gone, and I doubt she'll even last the month of July. In August, she'll go back to college, and we'll say we'll write or that I'll come visit, but that won't happen. This is it for us. Chandler will be like all the other girls I thought were my friends in high school who I'll probably never see again.

Dr. Blair, Sarah's father, comes in to pick up his order without his ticket stub and leaves his Volvo running. Chandler gives him a wave and goes back to tagging. I guess they see each other all the time, and it's not a big event that he's here at the dry cleaners. I find our copy of Dr. Blair's ticket and walk to the back to get his clothes. I press the button that revolves the dry clean ready-for-pick-up-rack *A-L*. The order is large—three dresses, six blouses, two pairs of pants. His new wife's order. I rip the carbon copy from the plastic sack and keep it in my hand with the original. "Fifty-eight sixty," I tell him. He gives me three twenties, takes the clothes, and hurries out without waiting for his change. Instead of stabbing the original on the silver spear like I'm supposed to, I stuff it with the carbon and the twenties deep in my skirt pocket. I walk to the register, open it, and close it. Chandler is still tagging. Nobody sees me, and I feel great. This is a victory. One for my side.

• • •

People say after the first time it's easy. Do it once, tell yourself it's okay, and you're fine. But for me it was easy the first time. Every week I'm taking at least fifty off the top.

The summer is over, Chandler is gone, and my mom has a job now with Penney's working at the makeup counter. She sneaks home moisturizers, eye creams, expensive face soaps, masks, and we try them out. I've promised her if I ever tan again, I'll do it slow and use sunscreen.

We're learning how to preserve.

I'm saving money, saving my skin, sleeping my weekends away, and soon I'll be ready for something, anything, who knows, maybe New York City.

Rhythm

October 1991

Sarah

So I'm going around the grocery store wearing this twenty-four-hour heart monitor. It looks kind of like a Walkman, and I have to hold it steady and low because there are these five electrodes stuck to my chest, and I can't make any sudden movements because that could loosen the electrodes and mess up the whole reading, and I'd have to do this all over again, and everyone is looking at me like I'm this pitiful freak.

I'm only twenty years old, if you can believe that, though my voice sounds even younger, like I'm fifteen or something, and when I've called to get appointments for the heart tests—the echo, the stress, the tilt table—the nurse is always like, "Oh, honey, nothing could be wrong with you, you sound so young," and I'm like, "Well, something's wrong because I have to come in."

My dad C. H. (Charles Henry Blair, but I started calling him C. H. when I was about six because he had these highball glasses engraved with a big, ugly *B* in the center, but with a very pretty *C* and *H* on either side) is this famous heart surgeon and said we have to be cautious and take all these tests because my EKG report from the emergency room came back abnormal, saying Possible Cardiac Infarction. But EKG machines, C. H. explained to me on the phone right after I was released from the hospital and called him, have a tendency to overread things, and he said that sometimes athletes have a slightly different heart rhythm and that I probably didn't have a heart attack but just had a little arrhythmia. "You know, Sarah," C. H. said, after I'd admitted to him that I'd had a fight with my half-brother Paul right before all this happened, "you ought to be calm and not fight with Paul or with me or with anyone ever again."

My cardiologist is a friend of C. H.'s, a *woman,* Dr. Stephanie Denny, an *attractive* woman whom I hope like hell he hasn't had an affair with. I sort of wish C. H. would just come up from Fort Smith, where I'm from and where he still lives, and practice in Fayetteville's hospital for a few weeks. C. H. as a dad is normally a jackass, but he's supposedly this incredible surgeon. And he's only an hour and a half's drive away. But maybe I'd feel kind of funny having him examine me.

I'm searching around for sick-people food—things like Campbell's Chicken Noodle Soup and soft wheat rolls and orange juice. I even get some stuff I don't like—grouper and oat bran—because it's good for your heart. Paul was supposed to go to the cardiologist with me and the grocery store and Blockbuster. If he were here to help, I might be already home by now watching a comedy or something, definitely not a thriller, eating bread and soup and being calm.

Instead, though, I'm feeling rattled trying to maneuver my cart without messing up the monitor. I know Paul is off drinking somewhere with his psycho friend Geoffrey, whom everyone calls Gee-off because we all live in Fayetteville, Arkansas, and are college students and think it's funny. He and Gee-off had an eight o'clock tee time, and he was supposed to be back by eleven, but it's like two in the afternoon, and I bet he's still not home.

At the register, my purse strap catches on the monitor, and I have trouble getting my billfold out, and the cashier has to help me.

"Did you just give blood?" she asks.

Like this is what people look like after they give blood. She's only about seventeen and really poor and scrawny looking, so I know I shouldn't judge too much. "No," I answer, "I just went to the cardiologist."

"Oh," she says and nods, but I can see she might not know what a cardiologist is.

I'll be happy when this twenty-four-hour period is up, and I don't *look* like a heart patient.

God, it's depressing being me. Old at twenty, Sarah Blair.

I decide to skip Blockbuster, and when I get home everything's clean, and that means the maid has come, and I'm really grateful that C. H. insisted Paul and I get one to come once a week because before the place was really a sty. Paul and I live together in this house C. H. bought for us because I hated the dorm, and Paul didn't want to live in some sorry rental. C. H. figures, too, that after we graduate, his other kids, a younger sister of Paul's who is also a younger half-sister of mine named Whitney and a couple of his stepkids we hardly know, can use it. C. H. has been married five times, and my mother is on her third marriage, and I have an older half-brother, Barry, from her, but he and my mother live up in Washington, D.C., where my uncle, C. H.'s brother, is a U.S. senator.

I take the groceries out of the sack and start putting them in the cabinet, and I feel chest pains, so I reach into my purse for the diary my cardiologist gave me and write down under time, *2:35 p.m.,* and under activity, *putting up groceries,* and then I write, *sharp chest pains (three of them).*

I don't have much of an appetite, but I'm thirsty as hell and drink two glasses of water, then sit at the kitchen table with a glass of orange juice. I'm trying to relax, but I only have a few sips before I stand up and slowly ease myself to my bedroom. I'm happy to see my room clean and my bed made, and I go into my spotless bathroom that smells of Lysol, and it's hard holding onto the monitor as I undo my pants and sit down.

I try not to look at myself in the mirror, but I can't help but look, and I have a kind of weird, sad face. And I'm wearing this pink silk blouse with pearl buttons that's really beautiful, but there are these wires that run out of the low-cut front and from the bottom that are attached to the monitor. I unbutton my blouse, and the electrode under my breast and closest to my arm feels a little loose because of lotion I probably shouldn't have put on this morning before my appointment. I dab my skin with tissue and try to secure the electrode. I start to cry, and I feel a jump in my heart, and I go and get the diary and write down, *2:50 p.m., looking in the mirror, heart jumps.*

I slip into pajamas, and that is no easy task, then finesse my way into my comfortable bed with my favorite yellow Ralph Lauren sheets the maid put on. I have the diary on the bedside table, and I look at it again. They give examples, so you'll know the kinds of things they want you to write down. One of the examples is *8:30 p.m., sexual intercourse, severe chest pain, heart pounding.* I don't know who on earth could possibly have sex with this monitor and five electrodes fastened to her chest but whatever. I guess you have to live your life.

Sex is what got me into this whole mess. Sex and the tennis team. Sex because I got pregnant by Gee-off and had an abortion and had a huge fight with Paul about him and about how he hits on me all the time and how it unnerves me. Paul defended Gee-off, saying he was harmless, because Paul doesn't know that Gee-off and I have slept together. Gee-off doesn't know I got pregnant. And, of course, Paul doesn't know because I went to Washington, D.C., to have the abortion, so I could get away and my mom could take care of me. Mom told me not to tell anyone about it, and I'm not going to, but Gee-off is confused about why I'm so cold to him, and Paul doesn't understand it either, and that is what caused our huge fight and my serious heart flutter and feeling like I was leaving the world and falling into a kitchen table chair and almost passing out and Paul lifting me up to take me to the emergency room. God, I was certain I was going to die.

In the car, I kept telling Paul how much I loved him and to tell C. H. and my mother and Barry and even Whitney (whom we both don't really like) how much I loved them. And to tell Chandler, my oldest friend, who goes to college at Sewanee in Tennessee, and whom I haven't even told what has happened yet because I don't talk to her often anymore, and I am afraid it will be too stressful calling her up and telling her I may have had a heart attack and could have died, then from telling her the story, have a heart attack and die.

And then because of the tennis team. I'd been drinking a lot with Gee-off and Paul and was hungover every day and miserable during practice, so before I left for D.C., I quit the team altogether. That was three weeks ago.

And when I got back, my coach and teammates tried to make me feel guilty about quitting and had this kind of intervention accusing me of being an alcoholic and drug addict. I haven't told C. H. yet about quitting, though maybe I won't have to ever with all this heart stuff. I'm not sure you can play college tennis, where you have to run lines and lift weights and sprint down the football field, if you have arrhythmia.

I slide my hand under my blouse and just under my bra and try to feel for a steady beat. I do that constantly. I still have this tightness above my heart all the time, but I don't report that in my diary.

I hear Paul come in, and he whistles two notes, the second one lower than the first, to signal he's home like he always does, and someone else mimics his whistle and, God, that must be Gee-off.

They come into my bedroom, ball caps on backward and drunk, and I'm always struck by how much Paul and I look alike, with our pale skin and dark hair, though half the time I color my hair blonde like Gee-off's. Strictly a coincidence.

"Have you been playing golf all day?" I say. "Because you were supposed to take me to the cardiologist."

Paul plays golf nearly every day at the Fayetteville Country Club. He walks around there like he owns the place. We don't even belong, but we can go and play tennis and golf because they have reciprocity with our country club in Fort Smith.

"Was that today?" Paul asks.

Gee-off laughs. "He's sorry, Sarah," he says and grabs Paul and pins Paul's arms back. "Here, I've got him. Whale on him. He deserves it."

"I deserve it." Paul grins. "You can have ten free shots. Come on. As hard as you can."

When we were kids and Paul would do something to make me cry, like make fun of my being slightly pigeon-toed when we'd play tennis, he'd present such an offer.

"Next time I have a heart attack," I say, "I'll take twenty shots. Now, leave me alone."

Paul holds his hands up, like he's surrendering, and steps away and leaves the room, but Gee-off steps forward and crawls under the covers from the foot of the bed and starts sniffing at my feet and up my legs like he's a dog, like he used to do. And I used to think this was charming.

He stops and throws the covers back. "What is all this shit you're hooked up to?"

"I gave blood today."

"What?"

"It's a heart monitor," I say. "You moron. Don't touch it and don't touch me. Get out of here."

"All right, whatever. I'm leaving," Gee-off says. "I need another beer anyway. Want one?"

"No," I say, reminding myself to be calm.

"Okay, then." And Gee-off rolls off the bed and finally gets out of my room.

Thank God I don't have to spend my life with Gee-off and a little Gee-off.

Instead of reaching for the diary, I try to breathe, slowly, deeply, quietly, and on the exhalation, "Ommmm."

. . .

Paul's been really nice this week. He hasn't brought Gee-off over once, and he returned my heart monitor and even went to the registrar's office and dropped all my classes. I'm really not in the right frame of mind to go to class and study, and C. H., who doesn't want me to stress out, told me, "Anything you don't want to do, you don't have to do."

What I do is take an Ambien that C. H. prescribed and sleep a heavy sleep and lie half-awake the rest of the day feeling my heart beat and watching television until my mom calls in the evening. I don't ever talk to her too long because if I do, then my chest starts hurting. She's trying to be strong and not cry, but it's hard for her so far away. She keeps asking if she can fly down, but I don't want her to. That would be a lot of stress having her stay with Paul and me, when Paul is not her kid and all.

. . .

I'm relieved Paul's already up this morning, sitting on the couch, drinking coffee, but when I see he's wearing a suit, I get nervous. I have on a big T-shirt and thin red sweat pants and tennis shoes because you're supposed to wear something comfortable.

"I'm ready to take you for your tests," he says. "The echo and the stress, right?"

"Right," I say and smile. Paul looks kind of funny in a suit because he's a clone of C. H., tall with rounded shoulders and a smug face like he's too cool and too liberal to be dressed up, and

I've never seen C. H. in a suit. I don't even think he wears one when he gets married.

"Going on a big interview this afternoon?" I say.

"A mock one," he says, "at Career Services. And it's gonna be taped."

He's got a couple of thick, boring-looking books stacked beside him, I suppose, so he can study while he's in the waiting room. He better. He's in his senior year, a business major, and barely has a 2.0.

"Good luck," I say.

"You, too," he says, standing up, and pats me on the back like C. H. does sometimes.

Fayetteville is a pretty hill town, and Paul and I live on top of a mountain called Mount Sequoyah, and to get to the hospital, we drive down windy, wooded roads. I look out the window and try to take long, even breaths, and Paul listens to sports radio.

There aren't many people waiting at the Heart Center—only a couple of stooped-over gray-haired men and one middle-aged woman. I go to check in, and Paul sits down, and I watch him pick up a *Modern Maturity* magazine. I take a seat next to Paul, and after a few minutes (C. H. must have some pull), the nurse calls my name, and I go in before the others.

The nurse gives me an I.V. that she calls a butterfly, I guess, because you can float around this place wearing it. It takes her two times to find a vein, then she realizes she has the I.V. going in the wrong arm and has to do it again. I'm trying to be pleasant. The nurse is young and pretty and seems so nervous. I hope it's because she's new and not because she, too, has had an affair with my father.

She leads me into another room that has a treadmill and an examination table next to the echocardiogram machine, which will take an ultrasound of my heart. When I had my abortion, I had to have an ultrasound, but I didn't look, and if there was anything to hear, I didn't listen. "You're eight weeks," the nurse told me then.

"Lie on your side," the technician tells me now. She's heavy-set and looks smart and serious. She rubs gel on my chest and stomach and moves this microphone around. I can hear my heart beating on the machine. It's so loud, you have to listen. I glance at the image, grainy and empty, then I see my heart, a black fist, which again disappears. I look at the pretty nurse, and she smiles at me.

I don't know what I'm most afraid I'll learn from these tests. To have to live my life like an old person with heart disease. To know I will die soon and have only lived in Arkansas. To have done nothing with tennis or with college. Not to have given anything of myself to this world.

Dr. Denny comes in. "Hi, Sarah," she says.

"Hi," I say. Almost a whisper. I want to ask Dr. Denny if she knows the results of my heart-monitor reading, but I'm too afraid. I hate feeling afraid.

The technician has me shift around, so she and Dr. Denny can get different views of my heart.

"Squeeze like you're making a bowel movement," Dr. Denny says.

God, this is humiliating.

"Like this." She bends her knees and makes a face like she's pushing.

I try my best. I want to believe she's never slept with my father.

"That's good," Dr. Denny says.

The nurse hooks me up to something that will monitor my heart rate and blood pressure, then helps me to the treadmill, and I start walking, easy and slow, but I'm scared because I haven't had any exercise in over a month, not since I quit the tennis team. The technician increases the speed, and I'm walking faster now and starting to sweat, and the nurse is asking me if I'm okay and talking about my target heart rate, which I don't really understand, like I can quit when I reach it or something. The technician increases the speed again, and I'm breathing hard and can feel my heart pounding.

"I think I need to stop," I say.

"Okay," the nurse says, "you've hit your target."

She and the technician rush me off the treadmill and back on the table, so they can take more pictures of my heart, and I start thinking about this big wicker basket we had in the utility room when I was young and C. H. and Mom were married. Paul and Whitney and Barry and I were all living in the same house, and everyone played tennis, and we would keep all our racquets in that basket, new and old, wooden and graphite, at least twenty of them.

"These look good," Dr. Denny says to the technician and the nurse and, I guess, to me. "I think everything's going to be fine, Sarah."

I can feel myself smiling, and I suddenly get my breath back, and my chest stops hurting, and I thank everyone, and the pretty nurse apologizes for screwing up my I.V., but I tell her I don't care and keep thanking her and the technician and Dr. Denny for how nice they've all been.

They look happy, too, and the nurse gives me a towel and shows me to the bathroom, and I wipe off my chest and stomach, but when I come out everyone's gone, and I have to give the towel to a nurse I don't know, and I find my way out to the waiting room and start crying when I see Paul, telling him I'm all right, that probably I'm all right.

"Only one test left," he says. "After tomorrow you're home free."

I smile, then I feel scared again because tomorrow is the tilt table, the test I've been dreading the most, the one where they strap you to a table and try to make you pass out to see if you have syncope, a condition where your blood pressure drops and you faint or almost faint, and I have fainted or almost fainted in my life many times.

. . .

You know, when I had the abortion, I didn't think of Gee-off at all. I thought about when I was young, playing tennis with Chandler at the country club. Groundstroke games to twenty-one where it doesn't matter who wins. To hit the ball as hard as you can and really get into a rhythm. I loved tennis back then. Especially in the fall, at night under the lights, when you could hear the cicadas, and it's fall right now outside, and I'm missing it.

The male nurse who's giving the tilt-table test says my blood pressure looks good and that I have a steady heart. He's surprised my EKG at the emergency room came back abnormal. He starts to tilt me up, just slightly, and I start to sweat and feel dizzy. "Are you going to pass out?" he asks. "I don't know," I tell him. He keeps tilting me up, slowly on an incline, and when I'm straight, I start to feel better. "You're fine," he says. "Just relax."

I was lying on a table wearing a paper gown during my abortion, and my legs were pushed up and open, and a doctor was probing inside, telling me to relax. I felt so light-headed and hot, and the nurse kept wiping my face with a cold washcloth. She had a trash can for me in case I needed to throw up. I felt a pinch and a sting and a ringing in my ears and a medicine taste, then for minutes, terrible cramping pain, and even with the machine-humming noise, the doctor kept asking me boring, personal questions like, "Where are you from?" and "Are you a college student?" I didn't answer. I couldn't because I fainted.

I don't faint here, and that is good news. That means I don't have syncope. I'm standing up, and I'm able to move my feet around and unlock my knees. "I normally work rehabilitating heart patients," the nurse says. "I haven't given one of these tests in years." Dr. Denny told me not to talk during the test. I just listen and look at the clock.

The abortion doctor said he got everything, and the nurse stuck a thick maxi-pad on the extra underwear I was told to bring, and I was able to put the underwear on myself, but she had to lead me to the recovery room, which was also a waiting room to see the doctor. I was still hot, and I saw other girls wrapped up with blankets. I was wrapped and freezing, too, before I went in. The nurse put me in a chair and tilted it back until I was stretched all the way out. She set a blanket on my lap and left the trash can on the floor next to me. Punk rock was playing from a boombox, and some of the girls who hadn't gone in yet were nodding their heads to the fast drum and bass guitar. And I thought of that Sex Pistols song, "She was a girl from Birmingham. She just had an abortion." A song Paul and I had screamed along to when we were drinking at home about to go out.

I have to stand here for forty-five minutes, and I've already gone forty. The nurse makes a phone call, and I hear him say that I'm fine, that I'm not going to pass out. He lowers me back down and unhooks me from the EKG machine, and I'm surprised because, compared to yesterday, this test is a breeze. He takes off my blood-pressure cuff and oxygen clip and I.V., and as he's unstrapping my chest and legs, Dr. Denny comes in.

I sit up, my legs dangling off the table, and the nurse lets her sit in his chair.

"All your tests are fine," she says. "And they didn't find *anything* on the heart monitor." She starts writing. "I'm going to prescribe you Klonopin. It will help with that tightness in your chest. And help you sleep." She looks up and taps her pen against her clipboard. "No more Ambien."

"Well, what happened?" I say. "Was it arrhythmia like C. H. thought or what?"

"Maybe," she says, "or a panic attack or a pulled muscle or all of that." She stands up and walks over and touches my arm. "I'll see you in six weeks, and we'll see how you're doing then." She gives me the prescription and leaves the room.

I hop off the table and thank the nurse, giving him a firm handshake, and I feel confident doing this, kind of like I'm my uncle, the senator, and the nurse leads me back out to the waiting room where Paul is slouched in a chair.

Even asleep, at least he's here.

C. H. calls maybe every other day, but he hasn't shown up yet, and he says Whitney is real worried about me, too, but she's never bothered to call. And neither has Barry. I wish I would have let my mom, who does call every day, fly down. Thank God for this pitiful Paul.

I lean over and punch him awake.

• • •

From now on, I will only play tennis if it's what I want to do.

The maples are the first to turn here in late October. Orange and red among the persistent green leaves of oak and elm. To see the orange and red fall on a freshly swept green soft court. To hear the wind in the trees mix with cars in the distance. To see the sun swell over the golf course.

Paul is trying his best not to be a hack, not to slice like he always does to try to break my rhythm and win a set. He's hitting deep and flat, and I'm swinging softly, for *me,* because I have to, since this is my first time out.

To hear the lights click on. To hear the whirring, chirping mating call of the cicadas who have shed their skin and grown wings. To see below the windscreen their abandoned shells still clinging to the chain-link fence from the dusk before. To take one in my hand, fragile and blonde and lifelike, and show Paul. To be the only ones here in this world.

SOUVENIR

Chandler

It's the middle of Saturday when the phone finally rings. I wait until the fourth ring to answer, expecting it to be Mitchell, my fiancé as of last Saturday. God, I hate the word *fiancé*. But it's Patrick, and he wants to open up the Union Theater, where he works, to see a lesbian art movie he's rented. Half an hour later he's sitting on my bed drinking a beer and waiting.

I look at Patrick as I brush through wet hair. "Just a minute," I tell him.

He lolls his head back and squints his eyes. "Whatever."

Patrick is twenty-one, my age, and tall, but he looks like he's gained a little weight, so he doesn't look as tall. Mitchell doesn't like Patrick. Mitchell says Patrick is mean to me, and he is sometimes, but I'm happy that Patrick called and that he's here, and when Mitchell calls, as he does every day, throughout the day, I won't know.

I sit on the floor to lace up my brown leather boots. Patrick scans me from head to heels and laughs.

"What?" I say. "You don't like them?"

"No, very hip."

He crosses the room to my bookcase and sways as he runs his fingers down the spines of my anthologies and novels and short-story collections and poetry. I'm waiting for him to say something.

40

"You're such an English major," he says and smirks. "So I'm guessing you've heard the rumors about my father for a long time and didn't want to say anything." He looks at me, and I go back to tying my laces.

I've heard people in the department talk about his father being a philanderer, but I didn't know if it was true, and I guess I didn't care. I've never had his father as a teacher, but I've seen him in the hall, always wearing a bow tie and walking in a hurry.

Patrick paces back to the bed, then sits hunched over, with his elbows on his knees. "This morning I'm at my parents' house, and while Mom's busy at church, at *church* mind you, I hear my dad in the study with his door closed talking on the phone. So I go to another phone and pick up, and he's on the line with some girl. I'm sure one of his students. And they're in high gear speaking Queen's English about how they need each other and fuck each other and shit. God, I'm the last to know, aren't I?"

He looks over, but I don't say anything.

"Oh, fuck it," he says. "I'm just glad it wasn't you on the phone. So, where's the ring?"

"I can't wear it," I tell him. Then I give an explanation about having to call a jeweler and how it will take a week to size.

"Really?" he says.

I stand up and look into his squinty eyes. "I haven't taken the ring in yet because I don't want to be away from it that long."

"Of course you don't," he says.

I suppose I should feel different since the ring. I wanted to feel different. I didn't want to hurt Mitchell's feelings by saying no, and I hoped my feelings would change. Two weeks ago Mitchell drove down from Nashville, like he does nearly every weekend, and proposed beneath Sewanee's enormous white cross, with the green valleys below, the fog, and when I accepted, I told him that at the end of the semester, after graduation, I would move with him to Memphis, where he'd begin working for a law firm overlooking the Mississippi River. But I knew that when I accepted, I would not move to Memphis. Not with Mitchell. Not with anyone. Heading back west and living in plain view of Arkansas is not something I could do.

"I don't trust lawyers," Patrick says. "They try to control people."

"Maybe you should be a lawyer," I say.

"Kara hates me," he says.

Kara hates me, too. Though I think she doesn't like me for the same reason Mitchell doesn't like Patrick. Like Patrick and I would ever get together.

"Now she won't even talk to me." He pauses a moment. "I'm high. It'll be good to see a lesbian art movie high." He sniffs twice, quickly, a tic he has sometimes when he's lying or nervous or angry. "I drink and smoke myself to sleep every night."

"Sure you do." I slip on my leather jacket and grab a lipstick, my license, and a twenty and put them in a pocket.

• • •

Patrick drives too slowly and keeps fiddling with the radio. There are CDs and CD cases scattered on the floor and in between us. In the backseat are empty beer bottles and spiral notebooks and about fifty golf balls and a putter and cleats caked with mud and dirty socks and a softball mitt.

"Can you drive all right?" I ask.

He twists his neck toward me. "Chandler," he says, "I drive better this way." He lets go of the wheel, and the car swerves, and I brace myself against the dashboard.

"God, Patrick."

"I know." He shakes his head. "My alignment's awful."

His window is rolled halfway down, and cold air rushes toward me. For a while we don't speak, and his hands stay on the wheel, but then he reaches for the ashtray and pulls out a joint. "We need this."

"No, thanks," I say.

"Come on." He parks in a space right in front of the theater, then lights the joint with a silver lighter on a low flame and takes a deep drag.

I'm ready to get out. "Do I need to lock the door?"

"No," he says, "my window's broken. It doesn't really matter."

"How'd that happen?"

He touches the glass, then lifts his shoulders. "Don't know."

. . .

The theater isn't really a movie theater. There's not a projector or anything with real film. It looks like a conference room, but with a bunch of chairs and couches and a giant TV screen and a VCR that Patrick runs. There's also a desk where he usually sits and does his homework while the movie is playing.

Patrick stretches out on one of the couches and puts his feet up on a chair and pulls out the joint he was smoking in the car. I sit straight on the other end of the couch, and it's dark and almost pretty watching the orange tip get shorter and him inhale with drama.

"Don't you want some?" he says. "You're all high and mighty now that you're getting married to Mitchell and won't do it." He laughs.

"Are you gonna turn on the movie?" I say.

"Oh," he says and flies to the back, and I hear him unsnapping the case and putting in the tape. Then the screen flickers and the previews start, and Patrick returns and puts his feet back up.

Mitchell doesn't like movies. He says he likes to read instead, to learn. But all he reads are books on politics and history. Books that have dates on all the spines.

The film finally begins, in black and white, and the first scene cycles four women's heads having a conversation about whether bisexuals are liars or just open-minded.

Patrick breathes deeply and sinks back into the couch and moves closer to me. "I love hanging out with you, Chandler. No one else would come here with me."

The screen shows different couples in a coffeehouse, and I start thinking about Mitchell's last letter. He wrote that he wished we were teenagers, then he would feel no shame in writing to me the lyrics of a song or composing a lame metaphor, comparing me to whatever he took to be beautiful. He had written that he had become too old and too serious to consider that a workable method. I was surprised and happy by his sentiment because I didn't even know he paid any attention to song lyrics.

Last year when I was home for Christmas vacation and looking on my dad's dresser for quarters to take back with me for laundry, I found a sheet of paper with the lyrics of James Taylor's song "Mexico." They were something like, "Oh, Mexico, I've never really been, but I'd sure like to go." And I was surprised to learn that maybe my dad had dreams of being something else besides a lawyer in Fort Smith, Arkansas. Maybe he dreams of being back here at Sewanee, and instead of being a political science major, being an English major like me, maybe of being me.

Sitting here in the dark with Patrick, I feel I am somehow betraying Mitchell.

Patrick leans into me. "I love just being in a movie theater. I always feel really cool."

"It's not really a theater," I say.

"Close enough," he says, "and it's dark."

"Yeah," I say. "People always look better in the dark."

"Well, we do."

I sit back and try to enjoy the film. It's kind of a sad story, a realistic story about a friendship between two women that ends when they try to make it into love.

As the film comes to a close, Patrick slaps the cushion between us. "I knew it would be over when they finally had sex. I figured it out."

I knew that, too, but I keep it to myself.

• • •

Patrick drums the steering wheel with his thumbs. "Let's go somewhere. I'm too sober."

"Pearl's?" I say.

He nods. "Yeah, Pearl's. Barbecue and beer. Great idea."

He whips out of the parking space, and I hear the beer bottles in the backseat fall to the floor and roll under me. They're clanging around, and I reach down and pick them up and throw them back where they belong with all his other junk.

"What did you think of the movie?" he asks.

"It was okay," I say.

"I really liked it," he says. "And, you know, it wasn't just watching women have sex. There was more to it. I identified with their timidness. Obviously, you're a little shallow, Chandler."

• • •

Pearl's is a really nice restaurant with fancy food, but they also have a barbecue shack out in the parking lot with picnic tables on a white gravel drive and under a big oak tree, and that is where we go. We order our food and a pitcher of beer, and while we wait at a table drinking, Patrick tells me what happened when he last saw Kara. "I just made her cry one too many times," he says and shakes his head and smiles.

They yell out that our order is ready, and Patrick jogs over and pays and sings in his Texan accent, "It's all on me."

I watch him gather napkins and forks, and I tell him to get

extra barbecue sauce for our sandwiches. He carries the tray over his shoulder like he's a waiter and sets it on the table, then jogs over again to the pick-up window and puts a five in the tip jar. "I always leave a good tip," he says loud enough for the guys inside to hear him.

He's right. He's a good tipper.

He keeps jogging, and when he makes it back to the table, he's out of breath, but still takes a huge bite of his sandwich. "God, this is living," he says and swigs his beer.

I open up my chips and eat a few.

"Eat your sandwich, for God's sake," he says.

I take a bite of my sandwich and wipe my mouth right after.

"So dainty," he says and tears into his chips. "Anyway, I saw Kara in the grocery store last week, over by the lettuce, and when she saw me, she just left her cart, man, full of groceries."

"She did?" I say. I don't believe this story, but I listen.

"She walked fast and prissy right past me, like I was going to leave my cart, too, and chase her." He slides the pitcher toward me. "Drink some more."

I shake my head. "No, I'm all right."

"Well, I could drink this pitcher and another," he says. "I just love drinking beer. Man, I love to drink beer." He pauses as if to reflect on the meaningfulness of beer, then takes an especially big drink. "Yow," he says. "Hey, let's eulogize." He lifts his glass. "Chandler. Reader. Divorcée. Friend." He nods. "Now, do me."

I can't think of what to say. I pause a moment, then clear my throat. "Patrick. Golfer. Moviegoer. Friend."

"Oh, come on," he says. He throws his arms up. "New game."

"No, I can do it." I lift my glass. "Patrick. Addict. Big tipper. Fraud."

Patrick laughs and clinks his glass against mine. "You know, we really hate each other."

"I don't hate you."

"Yeah, but you have." He takes a drink and shakes his head furiously as he swallows. "And I hate that pretentious, phony, impressed-with-every-little-thing Chandler bitch more than anyone in the world."

We're silent for a moment, and he finishes his sandwich and chips, then balls up his trash and shoots it into a wire can. I finish about half my food, wanting to eat all of it, but not wanting Patrick to watch me eat, so I push my plate away.

"Let's make out," he says. "I have the urge to lean over and just start making out. I feel a lot of love for you."

"No, thanks," I say.

"*No, thanks?*" he says and sniffs. "What's wrong? You miss Mitchell? You lonely? Well, let me tell you, I'm the one who's lonely."

"You are not," I say.

"I wish it were darker," he says. It's not quite evening, and he tilts his head back and looks at the sky. "You wanna get some fireworks? God, I'd love some fireworks."

"Okay," I say. "But I'll drive."

●   ●   ●

Sewanee is an isolated school with only one road leading out. We head toward I-21, but before we're really on our way, Patrick has me stop, so he can get a six-pack for the trip. The fireworks stands here in this part of Tennessee, in the Cumberland Mountains, are nothing like the little sheds you see pitched in Arkansas. They're as big here as truck stops, with marquees that loom above them twice the size of any billboard.

I turn off at Fireworks City, just as the flashing neon signs light up for the night.

"*Sale, sale, sale,*" Patrick says, reading the signs, as I ease into a space. He pops open a fresh beer. "We're definitely at the right spot."

"Yeah," I say, remembering stopping here with my parents on the drive to a tournament in Macon, Georgia, when I was thirteen and a tennis star, in July before the Fourth, when there was no sale. I've passed it with friends from Sewanee, on our way to Chattanooga for some action, but this will be my first time back.

Patrick offers his beer to me, and this time I take a long drink, and he takes a drink, and we do this like a ritual until it's empty.

Money is apparently no object to Patrick when buying fireworks. He fills a basket with bottle rockets, Roman candles, firecrackers, and a deluxe rocket with red, white, and blue streamers that alone costs sixty dollars. And he tosses in smoke bombs, snakes, parachutes, and sparklers for me, and his generosity reminds me of my father, and I remember my father, and me as a little girl, right here, at this stand, loading up on everything.

On the drive back to Sewanee, Patrick can't keep his hands off what's in the bag. "Firecrackers, man," he says. "I like to twist three or four together by their fuses, so they will really pop. Roman candles," he says, and shows me five varieties in different colors. "And for little Chandler," he says, "we have pretty parachutes and shiny sparklers."

We drink the rest of the beer, well, mainly Patrick does. The road curves and falls and rises and is full of truckers, and I have to concentrate, but I have a swig here and there, and we listen to a Hank Williams CD to really get us into the spirit.

Patrick says that the best place to shoot the fireworks will be over at Courts by the pond. "It's the best place," he says, "because Courts is a sucky dorm, and it's very dark and wooded, and there's a pond there."

We go there, and it's quiet, I guess, because it's still early in the night before parties and dates will begin. I park the car, and

Patrick jumps out with his huge sack of fireworks and runs ahead of me.

"Over here," he says, but I can see him, and he makes some bird calls, first an owl and then a whippoorwill. He's already lighting bottle rockets, a handful at a time. He waits until the fuses hit the powder, then throws them as they're flying out of his hand.

"Is that safe," I say, "throwing them in the woods like that?" I sound like my mother, how she used to worry about my father and me with fireworks.

"Oh, yeah," he says and smiles. "But if it will make you happy." Then he tosses a bottle rocket into the pond, and it's cool watching the fire dart beneath the water and pop with a whisper.

I reach into the bag and get my sparklers. Patrick lights one for me, then one for himself, and we write our names in the air. Patrick throws a few smoke bombs, and they smoke green and orange and pink and smell of sulfur. I light a parachute and step back, and I'm startled by how loud it is, and Patrick cheers and runs out to retrieve the green army man dangling from a patch of white cloth and gives it to me, saying, "Souvenir."

Then we start to hear kids from Courts yelling out their windows, and we decide we better get going before the campus police arrive. We walk calmly and deliberately over to the SAE house, the bag of fireworks still half full in Patrick's arms, the deluxe rocket rising out the top. He figures his legendary drunk and screw-up status will only increase there after this stunt. Patrick used to be a big-time SAE but doesn't live there anymore and has quit, kind of like me with Tri-Delt, though I quit after only a semester. Benedict, the dorm where I live and have a nice private room, is right across the street and will be our safe haven after we shoot off the rocket.

Patrick surveys the land, and we go to a really dark spot in the lawn with a clearing above between the trees. It's a little cold, but there's no wind, and the stars are bright. He pulls out the deluxe red, white, and blue rocket. He removes the cone, and he calls me over to look down the cylinder and see all the powder. We nod at each other, then he twists the cone back on. Along the sides are blue wings like what you'd see on a dart, and at the base there's a big red fuse.

"Here we go," Patrick says and lights it and steps back and puts his arm around me, and we watch.

A shot of light spirals up quickly and explodes loud and high in the air. Streams of red, white, and blue, and even yellow, a surprise, spray like a fountain for what seems like minutes. We hear whistles and claps coming from the SAE house, and I get scared, worried about the campus police, so I take off toward Benedict, Patrick running slowly behind me, still facing where the fireworks fell. We run through the dorm courtyard, passing bewildered students, and make it to my room, out of breath, and raise our arms, then shift our shoulders, until we are dancing, and we have never danced together, and we realize this, and we stop.

I take off my jacket and fold it over a chair, and my lipstick, tangled in the parachute, falls to the floor.

"Where's that engagement ring?" Patrick says. "I want to see it."

"All right," I answer, and I kind of glide to my dresser, then reach for the box. I can feel Patrick close to me, his breath heavy on my neck. "The diamond's small," I say. "Don't laugh at it."

"Like I could afford to buy someone a ring. I won't laugh." He takes the box from my palm and opens it. "Wow," he says.

I can tell he means it.

"It's beautiful. It's classic, not gaudy or anything." He rubs his finger around the gold band, over the diamond. "Can't believe you're getting married."

I slip the ring on my finger and push it down as far as it will go.

"I can't believe someone gave you something like that," he says.

"Me neither," I say, and I laugh.

"I'm serious," he says. "You're not really going through with this, are you?"

"Maybe, baby," I say.

"I don't want you to get married."

I glance up at him. His eyes are mean and still, and he turns away.

"I'm leaving," he says.

"I'm sorry about your father," I say.

He grabs his sack of leftover fireworks. Then he leaves.

I think about following him. I open the door and watch him pass through the courtyard, and because he stops slouching, I feel that he knows I'm watching. I step back inside and shut the door.

I pull the ring off my finger and hold it. It's a nice ring, and I'm glad Mitchell gave it to me. I wish Mitchell were moving to Washington, D.C., and not to Memphis. He'd like Washington. He loves politics. And I'd like it there, and maybe I could work on Capitol Hill. I have connections there, friends there. I'd like to move to a city, an international city, not to Memphis, a big sprawling town of country people. More of the same.

I lay the ring on the dresser, put on my pajamas, wash my face, brush my teeth, and get into bed. I'm about to call Mitchell, but then I think I'd better check my messages to see how many times he's called and if he's worried or mad about my being gone all day. But as I'm reaching for the phone, I see the light is not blinking, that I have no messages, that Mitchell never called. That no one called all day except Patrick.

A Matter of Someone Leaving

Chandler

This is the first time Scott Foster has ever talked to me. I'm sitting at my desk in the mailroom, sorting letters for Senator Blair, the senior senator from Arkansas, when Scott hooks his hands around the door frame and leans in. "Do you want to go to the Senate floor?" he says. "I have to meet the senator, and since you're new to the office, I thought you'd like to come with me."

Scott seems so cool, relaxed. He's wearing a softly wrinkled shirt with the sleeves rolled up. I feel his eyes looking me over. "Yeah. Sure," I say.

We take a subway that's for senators and their staff from the basement of the Dirksen Building to the Capitol. We flash our IDs to an elevator operator, then to a woman at the cloakroom where the senator is waiting for us. Scott hands him a chart and some papers. I shake the senator's hand. "Good to see you, Chandler," the senator says. He turns to Scott. "I know her father, Ben Carey. She comes from good stock." I smile. I picture my father in his lawyerly suit and wire-rimmed glasses. I am glad the senator thinks of me as my father's daughter. I want to say something about my father or growing up in Arkansas or at least about my best friend, Sarah, his niece, who got me the job.

52

I just want to say something, but I freeze. I feel scared and elated being so close to the senator. He smiles at me and puts a hand on Scott's shoulder and says, "Scott, my old boy."

On the way back from the Capitol, on the Senate subway, Scott sits across from me. He leans toward me, looking into my eyes. It's something the senator does, something all politicians do, part of their magic. They look at you like you're the most important person in the world, but Scott is telling me about his girlfriend. And I almost believe he's talking about me.

He and his girlfriend are going to travel through Asia for six months. She's already quit her job and is living with her parents in Connecticut. He's quitting his in a month.

Scott says that both he and his girlfriend grew up in Connecticut. I imagine him coming from an upper-class northeastern family, living in a tasteful house in a clean and rustic neighborhood, taking the train into Manhattan.

In the mailroom, the fax machine always hums, voices rattle. It's easy to fall into a daze opening, stapling, and sorting envelopes. I touch Scott's name on his box and trace each letter with my finger. I like how the two *T*s feel connected.

The senator said I came from good stock, which I guess is true. I graduated from Sewanee and majored in English, and I'm a good writer. The administrative aide, who hired me upon Sarah's recommendation, told me I was overqualified for the mailroom, but if I worked hard, then I could move up to legislative correspondent. It was just a matter of someone leaving.

• • •

I start dropping by Scott's office, which is not much bigger than a cubicle. There's a small TV in the corner, and taped on the walls are quotes in his own writing and a map of the world. I find any excuse to talk to him, acting interested in his issues. He's the housing aide and is working on a rural homeless bill.

"You'd be surprised," he says. "They're living in chicken coops, under overpasses. There are no funds for the rural homeless."

Scott eats lemon drops from a package on his desk.

I reach for one in a casual way and look at one of the quotes taped to the wall.

He who learns must suffer. And even in our sleep, pain that cannot forget falls drop by drop upon the heart, and in our own despair, against our will, comes wisdom to us by the awful grace of God.

"Do you like that?" Scott says. "That's the ancient Greek playwright Aeschylus."

"I do," I say, but I'm embarrassed that I've never heard of Aeschylus. I look at the map and finish off my lemon drop. "I'd like to go to Indonesia."

He looks at me and smiles. "You should go."

I fold my arms across my chest and shift my hips to one side, swaying slightly. "I still haven't really seen Washington. I've only been to museums and receptions on the Hill. I don't even know anyone who's not a staffer."

"I know a lot of great places," he says. "Have you been to Garrett's? It's kind of a neighborhood bar in Georgetown."

"No." I take another lemon drop and pop it in my mouth, then look his way. "Would you want to go there for a drink after work?"

For a moment, he cocks his head at me. "Yeah, okay," he says. "Okay."

· · ·

Garrett's is crowded, and Scott and I sit at the bar. We drink gin and tonics and listen to the Stones' *Hot Rocks* CD playing on the jukebox. I want to talk to him about work, but it's too loud for a real conversation.

After our third drink, he rubs his hand on my wrist. "So, what do you think, Chandler?"

"It's great," I say. My head feels light. I'm leaning close to him, my leg brushes against his. "Georgetown's a great neighborhood. Do you live near here?"

"I live back by the Capitol. Do you want to go there?"

That isn't really what I'm asking, but it's what I want to happen.

He makes a move to leave.

I put a hand on his leg. "Do you like your job?"

"Of course," he says. "I'm afraid to leave. I've worked hard on that bill for three years. I want it to pass."

"Do you think I could do your job?"

He pauses a moment and shrugs. "Maybe."

• • •

In his bathroom, I notice a ponytail holder and a red barrette on the floor behind the toilet. I look under the sink and find an empty box of Tampax and a woman's disposable razor.

He waits for me in the bedroom. A pair of running shoes and a headband are sitting on top of a big cardboard box marked Claire. "Who's Claire?" I ask. But I know who she is.

"My girlfriend," Scott says.

"She's a runner?"

"Yeah, marathons."

He pulls me toward him and kisses my neck, then my mouth. I feel his tongue, soft and wide, and a shuddering passes through me. We move onto the bed. In a quick sweep, he has my blouse off my shoulders and my skirt and underwear down, moving them off my ankles. I open my legs, and he pushes himself inside, making me jerk at the suddenness. My eyes are open, but I can't look at him. My gaze is fixed on the running shoes and headband on top of the brown box. I imagine Claire in a warm-up suit watching us, her head tilted to one side, crunching on an apple.

* * *

Scott strolls into the mailroom the next morning as if nothing has happened. "Hey, Chandler. How are you doing back here?"

I keep my head bowed and slice open an envelope.

"Do you want to go downstairs for some coffee?" he says.

After I left him last night, it was late and dark and nobody was on the street. I was afraid walking alone, not quite sure where I was going until I saw the dome of the Capitol and knew Union Station was not too far away, where I could get a cab to take me home.

"No, thanks," I say.

"How about lunch?"

I clutch the stack of letters in front of me. My hands feel wet. He says, "We could go to Union Station."

"Listen," I say in a soft voice. "You don't owe me anything." I turn around in my chair to look him in the eyes, like politicians do. I want to let him off the hook if he wants to be off the hook. "It was my fault as much as yours. We both had too much to drink."

He looks away from me, though doesn't turn his eyes completely away, as if he is studying the part in my hair.

"Don't worry," I say. "I won't tell anyone what happened."

Scott leans over me. His voice is soft, too. Everyone in the office knows about Claire. "I had a good time last night. I like you. I've been thinking about you all morning." He runs his hand down my arm. "Did you have a good time with me?"

I nod.

He smiles in a sly way. "So how about lunch?"

"No. I don't think I'll have time. Too much mail."

He looks down at his shoes. "Are you doing anything tonight?"

I say, "I don't know." And I don't know what I want.

"After work we could get take-out and rent a movie."

"Well," I say. I love movies. "If I can pick the movie."

He smiles. "Deal," he says, and my eyes stay on the doorway after he leaves. I think about the evening before, riding with Scott past the White House. The sun was setting, a yellow glow between us.

.   .   .

In front of Scott's apartment, a homeless man asks Scott for change. Scott doesn't give him any, but he speaks to him, saying he's sorry.

"I can't afford to give them money every time they ask. But I always talk to them," he says. "So they know they're alive."

I'm not sure how to respond. He sounds condescending, like many members of my country club back home sound when talking to the people who serve them. But I know he has good intentions.

Scott lights candles, opens red wine, and we eat Thai food (my first time, but I don't tell him that). After dinner, watching my favorite Woody Allen movie, *Hannah and Her Sisters,* I lie on the couch, and Scott sits in the chair and laughs in all the right places. The first time this has happened for me on a date.

"Do you want some more wine?" he says.

I run my fingers through my hair. "Please."

He takes my empty glass and goes into the kitchen.

"Hurry up," I say.

He yells over, "Nobody, not even the rain, has such small hands," a line from an e.e. cummings poem that is a line from the movie.

I answer with another line from the movie, "If Jesus came back and saw what's going on in his name, he'd never stop throwing up."

"Yeah, I love that actor. He's in a lot of Bergman films."

"Max von Sydow," I say, feeling smart.

"That's good," he says. He hands me a full glass and leans toward me and stops smiling to kiss me.

I pull away.

He bends down on one knee. He looks at me. "I thought about you all day."

"You did? How so?"

"We only have one month," he says. "I don't want to waste a single minute."

·   ·   ·

In his bed, after making love, he rubs my back. His hands move down my arms, then again to my shoulders.

"I'm nervous about the trip," he says. "I don't know how I'm going to act with Claire."

"What does Claire look like?"

He moves to get up. "I don't know."

I grab his shoulder and pull him next to me. "What does she look like?"

"She's tall with long brown hair," he says.

I lift my head up from the pillow and turn toward him. "Tell me about her."

"She's a lot like you. Pretty, intelligent, athletic."

I stretch my legs out as far as I can. My knees lock. I think about walking with my roommate, Paige, whose legs are much longer. I have to move faster to keep up. "I'm not athletic like Claire's athletic," I say.

"Oh, I thought you were."

"I play tennis. I don't run marathons." I lean back against the pillow. "I used to have long hair. It was to the middle of my back."

Scott closes his eyes. "I love long hair."

We lie still. After a moment, I say, "Send me a postcard."

"Oh, yeah," he says, and he seems sincere. "I'll send you post-cards and gifts all the time. Maybe some jewelry from Bombay. A necklace or something. Or silk pajamas from Singapore."

·   ·   ·

When Scott is in the mailroom sending a fax, I feel his eyes wander over my face, my hair, my dress.

He calls me from his desk and tells me to meet him at the watercooler. "I just want to be next to you," he says. "We don't have to talk."

I walk down the long hall, past his office, past the reception area, to the watercooler. I pull a paper cup from the dispenser and wait for him.

I watch the thin blue lines on his oxford shirt as he bends over to fill his cup. I sip my water until he turns to leave, until I feel him brush against my linen blouse. This is what I remember from the beginning: waiting at the watercooler and imagining how the lines on his shirt would feel against my fingers.

Scott and I go to movies he wants to see before he leaves. In the movie theater, my mind doesn't register the images flashing across the screen, and I never hear what the characters say. I turn to Scott, but he looks straight ahead. He's in another world. He doesn't reach for my hand.

At a dark, quiet restaurant, we sit in the corner by a window. Our table is small and round with a white tablecloth. We have already eaten, and our plates have been cleared. A candle fluttering in the center casts an orange glow, shadowing Scott's face, making it flawless. I hope that mine looks the same. I stare at his blue eyes.

"Do you have to go on the trip?" I say.

"I'm coming back, though. I'll see you when I get back."

I run my fingers along the rim of the glass holding the candle. "What about Claire?"

He looks off a moment. "I don't know."

He reaches for my hand, but I pull away. "You really have to go?"

"We've been planning this for a year. Claire quit her job." His voice grows faint. "You know that, Chandler."

I look at him. "So, is this it?"

He turns from me to look out the window at people walking by in raincoats and under umbrellas. "I really care about you," he says. "We care about each other, right? I'll see you when I get back."

I think about saying, *I think I'm in love with you. I could be falling in love with you. I'm scared I might be in love with you.*

Outside it's raining, and it seems perfect. Like a scene from a movie. Water will drip down our faces. My mascara will run.

"I love you," I say.

He opens the car door for me. "I love you, too," he says. "We just have bad timing."

. . .

The image of Claire looms everywhere. Sometimes I think of her in bed with us, the ridges of her running shoes pressing against my ankles.

After a while, we stop going out. Scott says he has to save money for his trip. "Every dollar I spend here," he says, "is forty-six rupees I can't spend in Bombay."

Every day work becomes more tense. Sometimes when I pass him in the hall, he won't look at me. He even turns his shoulders to one side to make sure he doesn't brush against my sleeve. He stops coming back to the mailroom, so I have to take him his letters at the end of the day. He doesn't stop typing when I set them on his desk. But still, each evening we leave together.

I follow him up the stairs to his apartment, my heels clicking against the wooden floor. "Why do you not speak to me all day, but then wait for me after work in the reception area? Why not sneak out the back door? Everyone in the office knows we leave together."

He closes the door behind me. "I don't know. Maybe they think I just give you a ride home."

"I know what they think." My voice is almost a whine, but I can't help it.

Scott paces, staying close to the door. "I'm sorry. I'm just confused. We have to stop sleeping together. I'm sorry. I'm not going to be able to handle it when I see Claire." He stares at me. "I have to spend six months with her."

"Fine. I'll get my things and go home."

"Chandler." He speaks to me with a gentle voice. "Is that all right?"

I nod.

"I'll take you home. I'm sorry. Sorry for everything."

On the way to my house, it starts to rain. He turns on the windshield wipers, but water still runs in rivulets down the front window. The only thing he says to me is that it is hard to see.

I run up the sidewalk, gripping my bag with yesterday's skirt and blouse and bra and underwear, and mail for the senator that should have been opened. I peer through the screen door, and my roommate, Paige, is ironing and watching television. C-SPAN, of course. I go in.

"Chandler Carey," she says. "Finally coming home."

I sort of smile and rake water out of my hair.

"Senator Blair was on the floor today," Paige says. "He was all alone, giving this impassioned speech to nobody, only to me, watching from the gallery."

I drop my bag and sit on the couch. She's ironing between buttons on a navy dress.

"He was great, going on again about that stupid mining law. Did you know that it dates back to 1872 and was signed by Ulysses S. Grant, intended to entice people to go west and settle?"

She doesn't notice that I might cry. I've never felt upset this way about anyone. Not even when I broke up with Mitchell. She's moving the iron faster than before, with bursts of steam and spraying starch.

"That archaic law permits mining companies to gouge billions of dollars of gold and silver and platinum from public lands without paying one cent to the American people, the *real* owners, the taxpayers, and we're required to pay billions of dollars to clean up the environmental mess left behind. It's an outrage." She sets the iron on the edge of the board and looks at me. "But I guess you know that."

"I've heard of it," I say. "And sometimes I get mail about it."

"Oh, and you have a letter from your dad, I think," she says.

I walk over to the kitchen table where we keep the mail. The table is actually an old door that Paige found and sanded and made a base for out of two boards, crisscrossing them, and painted white. It looks pretty good.

"And your mom called again," she says.

I hold the envelope. This is the first letter I've ever gotten from my father. I open it, and there's a check and a short note written on law-office stationery.

> *Dear Chandler,*
> *You got it done! There you are in Washington, D.C., working on Capitol Hill. It fills me with love and pride. Let's you and I try to correspond often. Your news will be more interesting than mine, but that's what happens to old folks. I wish I could swap places with you.*
> *Enclosed is a little walking around money.*
> *Love,*
> *Dad*

I fold the letter, with the check, back into the envelope. I'm glad he's in Arkansas and not here, seeing the place I'm in.

. . .

The next day at work the administrative aide calls me into her office to tell me I will be taking over Scott Foster's job. I will get a big pay increase, and I will have my own office. She tells me Scott has come in several times to talk about me. Scott wants to make sure the rural homeless bill gets passed. Scott doesn't want all his hard work to go to waste. I am smart and care about the issues, Scott has said.

I walk down the corridor, past the watercooler, to Scott's office. I stand just inside the doorway. The walls are bare. He sits in his chair, cleaning out his desk drawers.

He sees me, points at the TV. "There's a chance the rural homeless bill will be up."

I watch for a moment. The Senate chamber is nearly empty. Nobody cares about the bill but him. The senator isn't there, and the bill is certain to be pushed back until after the August recess.

"I got your job," I say.

He grins, pushing to his feet. "That's great. I knew it would work out." He walks over to me. "You're not going to let me down, are you?"

"I don't know," I say.

He brushes my hair behind my ear. "I'm sorry things got so bad."

"Me, too," I say.

"I want you to take over for me," he says. "You'll be my connection to the office."

. . .

Because I have his old job, I have his old connections. Every time I call HUD someone always tells me what a great guy Scott Foster is. I tell them he helped me get this job. "We are close friends," I say. "He's probably trekking in Nepal right now." I'm telling them more than they want to know, but I can't help myself.

A postcard addressed to the entire staff is passed around the office. It's of a man and woman running down a white beach in their bathing suits. A deep blue ocean is in the background. They are holding hands. BALI BALI BALI in red letters lines the bottom. *All this and a hut for only five dollars a day. Wish you were here, Claire and Scott.* The letters are small and slanted to the left. Scott's writing.

On the corner of Twenty-seventh and P, I think I see him. A man in a raincoat with his head down. Scott didn't even own a raincoat, but there is a striking resemblance. Barely slumping shoulders. Light brown hair.

It's almost fall now, my birthday has passed, and I begin to take in a lot of movies. I need them. I pay attention to what the characters are saying, attaching significance to every word, trying to understand what I'm feeling.

When I think back to those weeks, to why I felt what I did, I recall the excitement of not knowing what would happen. I kept thinking that for him, it was just an affair. Something temporary, to fill in time. But for me, it was different, I think. I felt a different way, and it had to do with him, but also with the not knowing. Uncertainty quickens the heart, fools you into believing what could never be true.

At lunch, I walk on the Mall and sit on the edge of the Reflecting Pool. I see my face in the dappled water, strewn with Popsicle sticks, wrappers, coins. A man sits, maybe twenty feet away, in old clothes with a stack of newspapers and smiles at me, and I smile back.

On the steps of the Capitol, there is a girl wrapped in a green pashmina shawl who's crying, and a guy is down on one knee looking up at her. I can't tell what he is saying, but it's not a marriage proposal. He's got the tone of voice of someone making an excuse for something. She's crying hard, not caring who's listening. I have to turn away, and I see the man in old clothes has folded one of his newspapers into a boat and is cradling it with both hands. He is smiling, but not at me, not at anyone.

A Winter's Daughter

Leigh

As I approach the railroad tracks, where the road dips and water always gathers when it rains, I grip the wheel to hold on, ready for the water this time to be frozen, and it's solid, not a sound of ice breaking, and my Honda begins to slide. I try to remember what Cassidy told me earlier on the phone when I was at work: *Stay calm and ride with the slide. Nothing sudden.* And I start to think about his proposal, a question just as casual as anything else he's ever asked: *So do you wanna be with me?* Then I turn the wheel too fast, obviously too fast because the car isn't turning, and I'm sliding into the next lane, bounding diagonally over the tracks, and no matter what I do with the wheel or the brakes I continue to go nearly sideways down Rogers Avenue into the opposing lanes, then slide off into a ditch in front of Blair Park.

I look around for somebody who might help me. It feels like midnight now instead of eight. The only headlights I see are my own, shining on frozen grass. Besides the rain, all I hear are my wipers packing ice at the base of the windshield.

I turn on my hazards, then wonder if I should get out and walk to the pay phone in the park. Blair Park is huge, twenty-six acres, and the phone is way on the other side, past the tennis courts and the miniature golf course, next to the pool and the train for kids. I try to see through the trees, through the darkness of so many of them, swaying and crackling, heavy with ice, and I decide to stay here and keep the heat on. I don't know who I'd call anyway.

Cassidy's band is playing tonight at Old Town, and I know Mom's at home in her sweats and dirty hair watching television in the dark. She's been that way for three days, since she got fired from Penney's for always being late because her car had to be started with two steak knives. You never knew how long it would take to get it going. Then the steak knives stopped working, and when the guy next door who's an expert hot wirer couldn't get it started, she had to call Penney's to tell them she wouldn't be coming in at all, but they didn't care and fired her. I'd like to think the people at Andre's, where I work, would be more reasonable, like how they let me go home early tonight because of the weather. They tell me I do a great job, but it's easy to do a great job selling fancy cheese and wine and whole-bean coffee. All things I'm learning to love.

I'm staring off toward the intersection of Rogers and Free Ferry when I see a truck with lights high off the ground coming in my direction. I put my hood on and have to throw my shoulder against the door to break the ice, and once I'm out on the slope of the ditch, my heels dug into the grass to keep from falling, I see that it's a blue Blazer and wave my arms, realizing that this is no stranger but someone I know. "Mr. Carey!" I yell.

He pulls parallel to me and gets out, wearing his green London Fog coat with the suede collar I recognize from when I used to work the counter at the dry cleaners. "Hi, there, Ben Carey," he says, walking to me, or swaggering as he does, with his hand out. "You need some help, young lady?"

I shake his hand, and I can't help smiling. "Mr. Carey, we know each other. I worked at Sunny Day Cleaners. I'm a friend of Chandler's. We were in the junior-high choir together. I spent the night with y'all once."

"Oh, yes."

"I'm Leigh. Leigh Ingram."

"Yes," he says, and his small, brown eyes get even smaller when he laughs. "Leigh, how are you?"

I laugh. "Not so hot, Mr. Carey."

He walks around to the front end of my car tipped down into the ditch, and he slips a little in his dress shoes and braces himself against the fender. He shakes his head. "I guess we better go to Exxon for a wrecker. I don't have anything to pull you out with myself." He steps around the car and reaches in to turn off the engine and lights, then shuts the door and climbs up to the road and hands me my keys and purse.

"Thanks, Mr. Carey."

"Here, let me help you in," he says, opening the passenger door of his Blazer.

With his hand on my back, I heave myself up and have to grab a package of Red Man chewing tobacco and a white styrofoam spit cup before I can sit down. He closes the door, and I try to find a place to set the tobacco and cup, but the center console is covered with a yellow legal pad, and a pair of gloves is in the cup holder. I notice the ashtray is pulled out and is full of change and golf tees in all colors, red, blue, yellow, and orange. I didn't know they came in anything but white.

He shakes the rain off his coat and hops in and has to turn the key twice before the engine starts. The heater is going full blast, and the radio is on with a Razorback basketball game. "Let's buckle up, Leigh," he says, reaching for his seatbelt. But I don't move, and he looks over at me and sees I'm holding his Red Man and spit cup. "Good Lord," he says, "I'm sorry." He takes them from me and tucks them on the dash in front of him, as I buckle up.

I think about how I used to see him at all the junior-high football and basketball games when I was in the pep club with Chandler. He'd always walk by carrying Cokes and popcorn for him and Mrs. Carey, and his hands would be too full to wave, so he'd just nod. He was so handsome back then, still is, though now his black hair is graying at the temples. I always wished if I ever saw my father that he would look like Mr. Carey. But my mom says my father is not handsome and never had any money and was always getting fired, and when she got pregnant, she knew leaving him in California to come back to Fort Smith, Arkansas, was the right thing in the long run for me. People sometimes ask if I've ever tried to find my father, but I haven't and don't want to. My mother is burden enough.

"So what are you doing with yourself these days?" Mr. Carey asks, though he doesn't look at me. He's leaning forward, watching the road, the window only half-defrosted.

"I work at Andre's," I say.

"Hey," he says, "I hear that's nice. I'll have to go in there sometime."

"Is Chandler still in Washington, D.C.?"

"No, she's at NYU Law School now," Mr. Carey says. "In her second year."

"Greenwich Village," I say. "She always wanted to go there."

He looks at me and smiles. "Sarah Blair is in New York, too, but they don't live together. Chandler says she'd never get any studying done if she had to live with her."

"That's true," I say. "Where did you go to law school?"

"Duke," he says. "Boy, I had to study, but some of those guys never did and played cards all the time and still got As. I wish I'd been one of them. They had a lot of fun."

I smile, and Mr. Carey looks like he's remembering something he might tell me.

"Leigh, you know, I lived in New York City when I was young, in my twenties. The firm worked me like crazy, but I had a great time in Manhattan going out drinking and eating steak and oysters and bread. Every place served really good bread before your meal. I hope Chandler's eating some of that good bread."

I wish I had something to tell him about somewhere I've been or anything at all to say.

We listen to the Razorback game for a while, and Mr. Carey says "damn" when the other team scores, and I stare out the window at the few cars going the opposite way on Rogers Avenue, watching freezing rain fall in front of headlights.

He turns his blinker on early, and when we come to the Exxon station on the right, he pulls in, and we slide to a stop by the office. "Stay warm," he says. "I'll take care of it." He leaves everything running and goes inside to speak to a man sitting at a desk with his feet propped up.

I watch Mr. Carey unzip his coat, and as he opens his billfold and takes out a card, the man at the desk lowers his feet to the floor and sits up. I can't say I'm surprised he's paying for me. Mr. Carey is just like that, I guess, and I'm relieved because I don't really have any extra money for something like this. I turn away and look down at the golf tees in the ashtray. I reach for one and roll it like a baton between my fingers, the way Cassidy has a habit of playing with a guitar pic. And as I do this, my eyes wander to the legal pad on the console, and I see it's scribbled with columns of numbers like he was adding something while he was driving, then I realize it's the same column of numbers all over the page, with the same total, over and over again.

Mr. Carey surprises me when he opens his door and gets in. "The wrecker's away right now. Have you eaten supper? We could kill some time at Wendy's there across the street."

"If you let me buy," I say.

"Oh, no, Leigh," he says. "That's out of the question."

"But I saw you pull out your credit card for the wrecker. You can't buy my dinner, too."

"Sure I can," he says. "I want to. Because you're a friend of Chandler's."

I smile. "Thanks, Mr. Carey. And if you ever want some really good cheese or coffee or anything, I could give it to you free from Andre's."

"Deal," he says. "Now, let's buckle up, Leigh."

"I'm still buckled," I tell him, though it seems kind of funny that he's so worried about putting on your seatbelt since we're only driving about fifty feet away.

He has to get into the turning lane quickly for Wendy's, and the car slides, and he holds his arm out to brace me, and we ease into a space.

We both have on our hoods walking into Wendy's, and both our coats are green, and Mr. Carey is holding his arm to steady me, and I'm holding his arm, too, because we are having trouble on the slick asphalt, me in my heels and Mr. Carey in his dress shoes.

Mr. Carey gets a large chili with a bunch of extra crackers and a large Coke, and I get me a chicken sandwich with cheese and mayonnaise, small fries, and a small Sprite, and we sit at a table by a window that faces Exxon, so we'll know when the wrecker's back. Our coats hang on chairs at the next table.

As I unwrap my sandwich, I watch Mr. Carey, neat in his gray suit and red-and-navy striped tie, smash his crackers, one package at a time, then tear each one open and sprinkle the crumbs in his chili. I wait for him to take the first bite, and he sees me waiting.

"Go ahead and eat, Leigh. It takes me awhile to get all prepared."

"Okay," I say, but I just eat a fry.

He reaches for the pepper and shakes maybe a dozen times, then reaches for the salt but only dashes on a little. "Leigh, when I eat chili, I like to pretend I'm a cowboy on the range and have just been called out of the bunkhouse for dinner. And I'm starving because I've had a tough day, rounding up cattle and killing rattlesnakes." He takes a big spoonful and opens wide long before the spoon ever reaches his mouth.

I keep watching him and bite into my sandwich.

"And if I were eating sardines," he says, then takes a drink of his Coke, "I might pretend I was living in Alaska in a cabin out in the middle of nowhere, and it was real cold, and sardines were all I could catch to eat."

I start thinking that I'm somewhere, maybe New York City, hungry, with no money, and I happen to find a five-dollar bill on the sidewalk and am able to go into the nearest Wendy's to eat this chicken sandwich.

"Chandler hates the smell of sardines." He laughs. "She hates the smell of a lot of things I eat. Leigh, I like to go home each day for lunch, and on my way I always stop off at Winton's Grocery and buy one can of sardines, one can of sauerkraut, one can of beets, and one can of spinach. Not the big cans, of course, but the smaller ones, like this," he says and holds his hand in the shape of a *C* to show the size. "And at home, I like to put each can into its own separate bowl, and this drives Chandler's mother crazy because she says I wipe out all our bowls at lunchtime. But you know, Leigh, I keep telling her to buy more bowls. You can never have too many bowls."

I laugh and remember what Cassidy says about Mr. Carey. Cassidy works at Movieland, and Mr. Carey goes in all the time and rents the same movies over and over again. *Zulu, The Man Who Would Be King, Lawrence of Arabia, The Untouchables.* Cassidy says they tell him he'd be better off just buying them, but Mr. Carey just smiles and says, "Nah."

We eat in silence, occasionally glancing over at Exxon to see if the wrecker's back, until we finish our meal. Then Mr. Carey goes to the counter and comes back with two medium Frostys.

"Mr. Carey," I say, "are you a lawyer like in the movies, in the courtroom and everything?"

"Not really," he says. "I used to be a corporate lawyer, but now I've got these two big personal-injury cases, and I'm working with a firm in St. Louis, and their lawyers are pretty slick. I do most of the research, take depositions, and I'll sit with them in the courtroom, but I won't give the actual performance like the lawyers do in the movies."

"Oh, okay," I say and nod.

"These cases, Leigh, with these cases," he says, his voice going to a whisper, "I have a chance to make more money than I've ever made." He lifts his eyebrows, his eyes real round and dark, and he clasps his hands together, almost like he's praying. "In my whole life."

I dip my spoon into my Frosty, and I can tell Mr. Carey is thinking about something, maybe those numbers I saw on the legal pad, maybe running those numbers again in his head.

He opens wide, keeps the spoon in his mouth for a long time, then slides it out and stands it up in his Frosty. "When Chandler was a little girl, about five, in kindergarten, the teacher told us that the kids were starting to make fun of her for how she talked. She had a lot of trouble with her *L*s and *R*s and with blend sounds like *Ch* and *Tr* and would substitute a *K* for any sound she couldn't say. It was around Christmastime, and they were singing 'O Christmas Tree,' and Chandler would say, *O Kismas Key, O Kismas Key*. And she'd sing it loudly because, of course, her mother and I would tell her she had a wonderful voice."

I laugh because I remember Chandler always being too shy in the junior-high choir to sing anything loudly.

"The kindergarten teacher told us we had to get her into speech therapy, and we did right away. We would take her twice a week to practice her sounds with Mrs. Zotti. And Mrs. Zotti said Chandler probably learned this from us, that we were reinforcing her at home. And we felt terrible because we were. She was such a beautiful little girl and so cute when she spoke. So Mrs. Zotti gave us these mimeographed sheets of pictures of the words Chandler was having trouble saying, and then we cut them out and put them on playing cards for her to practice with, and we would each have a hand, like in poker, and we would draw from each other and say whatever the picture was on the card. Chandler loved playing cards. And, Leigh, we did this every evening for months, from Christmas, I believe, until the spring."

I smile but feel sad. My mother has never done anything every day for months for me. Cassidy will call every day, and that's as close as it comes.

"And then early one morning," says Mr. Carey, sitting up straight and gripping the edge of the table, "she came into our bedroom and woke us up. She was standing at the door." His voice begins to break. "And she said, Leigh, with such sweetness and clarity, 'Yel-low. Law-yer.'" His eyes water, and he grins. "You should have seen how happy she was, and we were. Chandler's mother clapped, and I whistled and waved my fist in the air," and remembering this, he waves his fist in the air.

And I clap. "That's a great story, Mr. Carey." In first grade, I was in the slow reading group, and I remember how embarrassing that was for me. And now Chandler is in law school at NYU.

Mr. Carey turns to the window, then taps it with his finger. "Lord, Leigh, the wrecker's back. No telling how long they've been waiting on us."

We both rise, and while I put away our trays, Mr. Carey zips his coat all the way up so that his suit and tie once again disappear. Then he helps me with my coat, and I button up and tie my hood.

"Thanks for everything," I say.

"You're welcome." He ties his hood tight around his face. "I've enjoyed this."

Outside, the freezing rain is turning to snow, small wet flakes that vanish when they hit the parking lot and the avenue but are building up white on cars and trees and grass.

"Leigh!" Mr. Carey says and points up at a street lamp, where the snow is coming down heavy and fast in the light.

"The light looks like a skirt, like a skirt of snow," I say and hold out my arms, and Mr. Carey laughs.

We stay like that for a moment, watching the snow and smiling, then we help each other to the car, and Mr. Carey opens my door, and I lean over and unlock his, and while the windshield defrosts, we rub our hands and hold them up against the vents. It's half-time, and the Razorbacks are ahead by five.

"Let's buckle up, Leigh."

"All right," I say and wonder how many times he's ever said that to Mrs. Carey or to Chandler, and now already three to me.

We drive over to Exxon and stop in front of the office.

"Okay, Leigh," Mr. Carey says, pointing past the wrecker into the garage to a guy in a baseball cap. "That fellow will take you to your car and tow you out."

"Thanks, Mr. Carey. Thanks a lot. And will you tell Mrs. Carey and Chandler I said hello?"

"I will," he says. "And you be careful driving home."

"I will," I say. I unbuckle and grab my purse, but I hesitate getting out. "Mr. Carey," I say, "I think I might get married. To Cassidy. You know him. He works at Movieland. Brown hair. It used to be long, and he'd wear it in a ponytail, but he just cut it, and now it's real short."

Mr. Carey nods, and I can tell he remembers him. "Oh, he's a nice boy, Leigh," he says. "I *like* him."

I open the door and wave at him before I shut it. I stand there a moment to watch the snow, then turn when Mr. Carey honks his horn and pulls out onto Rogers Avenue. I wave again to him and start walking to the garage, putting my hands deep in my pockets. And I feel something, like a pencil, stick me in one of my knuckles, then I realize it's the golf tee I was playing with earlier, rolling between my fingers. I didn't mean to take anything from Mr. Carey, but I'm happy to have it and hold it tightly, hoping it is yellow.

Sarah Plus One

Sarah

I was already feeling lonely on my birthday at three this morning at Lakeside Lounge and convinced Chandler to sleep over.

The radiator is hissing and clanging, like somebody down below is hitting the pipes with a baseball bat, but Chandler manages to sleep, perfectly still and silent beside me on top of the covers, blonde hair swept off her neck. I almost feel like we're kids back in Arkansas sharing a room at some Hilton somewhere for a tennis tournament, and I'm almost comforted by this, until I remember how Chandler's mother would chauffeur us around and sleep in the bed beside ours, how her mother loved Chandler and never missed a match.

I feel depressed and get out of bed to have some Evian, then brush my teeth, but I still have a dry, horrible taste in my mouth. Maybe it's just hangover depression, but probably it will increase as the day goes by because I'm sure I won't hear from my half-brother Barry or my half-sister Whitney or even my dad, C. H. There's a shot with my half-brother Paul, if he remembers, but his memory isn't great. My mom will call sometime today, but she's always late with the card and the birthday check, and C. H. just blows it off completely, saying he gives me so much money that he feels like it's my birthday every day.

C. H. can't get over the rent and how much everything costs

day-to-day in Manhattan. Every month when he gets his credit card statement (I get a call then), he says he's baffled by how much I'm spending, and I say, "Hey, I'm just living."

I look out the window, and the sun is bright on all the buildings, as though it's in them. I feel a little better and glance at the clock and see it's almost eleven. Maybe I'll walk to SoHo and buy myself a present, maybe a new pair of shoes. New York's hard on shoes.

I nudge Chandler awake, and she smiles, says, "Happy birthday, baby," and closes her eyes again. When we were in high school and first dreamed of living in New York, we thought we'd drink daiquiris at every meal and all our friends would call us baby.

"I'm going out awhile," I say. "Stay as long as you want. Stay the whole weekend if you want." I throw on jeans and this T-shirt I have that says "Lucky" because I need it with my life. "Thanks for staying out late," I say.

Chandler opens one eye.

"You missed Evidence class," I say.

"Oh, it's all right," she says. "There'll be another one Monday."

"Right," I say. I skip class all the time. A lot of people do, but when they show us on Bravo, *Inside the Actors Studio* with host James Lipton, everyone acts so scholarly, asking questions. James Lipton's all right. I talked to him at a party once, and he told me his wife was Miss Scarlet on the Clue game. As kids Paul and I loved that game, but we didn't have anybody else to play with, so we'd each play two or three people. But every time he'd just have to be Colonel Mustard. And I'd just have to be Miss Scarlet, waving around a red Papermate pen like it was a cigarette holder. Man, I loved it when she did it with the candlestick in the Conservatory.

Chandler's in her second year of law school at NYU. I wouldn't have had the courage to come to New York and apply to the Actors Studio Drama School if she weren't already living here. She even wrote my recommendations, just took hers and changed law school to acting school, and personal essay, fake stuff like my wanting to be an actor all my life and my being Anna in *Burn This* at the Hardscrabble Repertory Theatre for the City.

I sit on the floor to put on my tennis shoes. "We still going to Brinson's show tonight in Hoboken?" Brinson Carr is this singer who Chandler dragged me to see one night, and after the show we started talking, and he's sort of become my boyfriend.

"Of course," she says and closes her eye, and I think she's already back to sleep.

I put on my purple coat I got in London, grab my purse, and I'm out the door. I start bounding down the stairs, six flights, and I start to feel happy and even happier once I'm outside in the sun. People are everywhere. They always are where I live on MacDougal Street, next to Washington Square Park.

I start walking and thinking about my birthday and last night and how the only gift I have is the one from Chandler. This shadow-box-looking framed picture of a yellow cab she bought on the street in Times Square because we take a lot of cabs together and because I really enjoy hailing them. Brinson hasn't given me anything yet, didn't even stay until midnight to wish me a happy birthday. He met Chandler and me out at the Lakeside for a couple of drinks, then said he had to go, that he was in the middle of working on a song, of course. Chandler loves his music. Says he's the best singer/songwriter there is, that his lyrics are even better than Elvis Costello's. He's good, but I don't know.

I get lucky at Houston Street and cross without having to stop on the median, and I keep walking to Prince, my favorite shopping street in SoHo. I'm looking through glass at this pair of boots and this guy touches my shoulder, startles me, and I turn around.

"Excuse me," he says. "You know, you're very pretty."

He looks like a Wall Street guy on casual Friday, with Giorgio Armani glasses he probably doesn't even need, a suede bomber jacket, and really blue jeans.

"Nothing personal," he says, "but I can tell already you're not my type, there's just no chemistry between us, but I bet you're the type to have friends I might be interested in, have the right chemistry with. What do you say?"

I step back toward the street.

"Watch out for that curb," he says. "I'm Adam, and your name?"

This is an odd situation, but I answer and hold out my hand. There is something harmless and likeable about him.

"Sarah," he says. He gives me a firm shake. "That's a good name, kiddo."

Kiddo? He's maybe three years older than I am.

"I'm a Scorpio," he says, trying to be funny.

"I'm lucky," I say and open my coat to show him, and he laughs. "Today's my birthday," I say. "I'm twenty-five."

"Today's your birthday?" He slaps his really blue jeans, and they sound starched. "Oh, let me buy you something. Why not? Give me twenty minutes."

"No," I say, "take twenty-five."

Adam laughs. "We have friend chemistry. I can tell."

"*I* can tell."

"I'll meet you back right here," he says, pointing at his feet. "Don't run away from me. You might find this hard to believe, Sarah, but most of the time I scare women off."

I smile and go into the shoe store, and I don't know how I feel, rejected as a woman, sure, not that I would ever like *him,* but I'm happy to have a new friend and get another present.

Nobody in here pays any attention to me. I look around, find a few options, and ask this French girl for help. She brings the shoes to me, all black, and I try them on and strut around, trying to kill time, but the woman is staring at me like I better buy something for troubling her. I finally decide on these flat-heeled boots that come up to my knees and will look good with a short skirt tonight for Brinson's show.

I give her the Sarah Blair American Express card that is really C. H.'s (I mean, he pays for it) and feel good when the transaction goes through. I'm always a little afraid C. H. is going to cut me off one day, make me get a job and teach me a lesson.

I walk outside and wait and wonder what Adam is going to buy me when I see him running up the street, waving something in his fist above his head, like he's Rocky or something.

He's wheezing when he reaches me. "I've got polyps and bad knees and a bad back and problems with my digestive system," he says. "I'm lactose-intolerant, Sarah, self-diagnosed."

"I'm sorry," I say. Lord, what do you say to that?

"That's why I'm late."

"Oh," I say.

"Here," he says and hands me this heavy round thing wrapped in pink tissue paper. "Happy birthday, kiddo."

"Wow," I say and begin to tear open the paper, and there's this glass paperweight with a flower painted inside. It's a pretty fucking cool daisy.

"I hope you like it," he says.

"I do," I say. I turn it over and see the stem. "I really do." I wrap the paperweight back in the tissue paper and put it in my bag with the boots.

"You've got pretty hair," he says. "Do you color it?"

"Yeah, at Brad Johns. Thanks," I say. "Hey, would you like to eat lunch?"

"Like to, kiddo, but can't." He reaches into an inside pocket of his bomber jacket and pulls out a monogrammed silver business-card case. "Got to go back to prison. Goldman Sachs. I hate it."

He gives me his card. It's ecru with a small, raised square on the right with the firm's logo in pale gold, and on the left is the firm's name and address and his phone and fax, all in black. It doesn't have his title on it or anything. Just Adam Kessler engraved in thick letters, the same pale gold as the logo. Then he hands me a stack of them, maybe fifteen.

"Next time you're at Brad Johns," he says, "would you pass these out to any blonde models you think I might like?" He puts his card case away. "Or maybe an actress. A friend of mine from work has been dating a girl from *Baywatch*. Long distance, of course."

"*I'm* an actress. *I* go to the Actors Studio. *And* my hair's blonde." I hold out my arms. "What's wrong with me?"

"Nothing, nothing at all, kiddo. That's why you can help me. And I can help you, too. Do you have any cards?"

I pat my coat where the inside pocket would be. "All out," I tell him, "but I'll give you my number." I unzip my purse and search for something to write on, but I can't find anything, so I use one of his cards and scratch out his name and number and write in my mine. "Here," I say. "Good as gold."

He looks at it and smiles. "Happy birthday, Sarah Blair."

I smile back and put the rest of his cards in my coat pocket. "For easy access. In case I meet a model or famous actress on my way home." I wave and walk away.

I don't feel like going home, so I pull out my cell phone and call my friend Shawn, who's in my scene-study class, to warn him I'm coming, that I'm on foot, but that I walk fast and will be there soon.

Open cabs are flying past me, but I don't even feel like hailing. Although, once I make it to Bowery, things don't look as pretty, and I'm tired of the fresh air and sunshine and sick of walking, but I press on until I finally reach the downstairs door of Shawn's run-down apartment building, and it's open, broken, so I don't have to buzz, and I drag myself up to 2D.

I hear Madonna playing and knock to the beat ("If you took a holiday"). Shawn throws open the door, and he's dancing, wearing orange-and-black Versace parachute pants and a camouflage shirt with the sleeves cut off, and singing ("oh yeah, oh yeah"), and he gives me his hand, and I follow him in, and he spins me around ("took some time to celebrate"), and holding me at arm's length, he suddenly stops singing and dancing and curls up his lip like he's Elvis.

"Yucky?" he says, staring at my chest.

"No," I say. I set my bag down and open my coat all the way.

"Oh, *Lucky*," he says and laughs. He turns off the music. "Happy birthday, Sarah."

I'm so happy he remembers, and he looks so beautiful that I want to kiss him full on the mouth, but instead I hug him tightly, and he's so small and fragile that I quickly let go and look around the room.

I haven't been to Shawn's in a long time, and it's more gay than I remember: a lot of glitter and disco balls, magazine pictures of Madonna and Marilyn and crosses and rosaries everywhere. He's not Catholic or anything, and right above the couch is a great big naked picture of Shawn himself but cut into puzzle pieces and arranged out of order. I've seen it before but never really checked it out—an ear, a foot, his neck. I keep on looking, what the hell, but I know I'm making a face like Elvis.

"Come on, Sarah, let's celebrate. The Mexicans are coming."

I follow him into the kitchen. "What Mexicans?"

He opens a new bottle of Absolut. "Kenny and Carlos, who make deliveries." He grins. "I think Carlos is in love with me."

I'm finally clueing in here on just who the Mexicans are. "Okay," I go, "I'm game."

Shawn doesn't have any tonic or any clean glasses, so we each take a swig from the bottle. We eye one another and smile and take another swig, and now I don't know what to say or what else to do.

I'm starting to feel a little nervous about this, thinking how years ago, back in college when I was living with my brother Paul and partying a lot, I had what felt like a heart attack and had to go to the emergency room. The first question this emergency-room doctor asked me was, "Do you do cocaine?" I had done it before, sure, but you couldn't say I was *doing* it. And I haven't done it since, even though, it turns out, my heart is healthy. It was just stress or panic, but I didn't drink or do anything for a long time after, just took my anxiety medicine, eventually started going back to class like I was supposed to, and began playing tennis regularly with this fifteen-year-old star player who reminded me of *me* when I was young and talented. Tennis and acting are all I've ever been good at, but I'm still a better tennis player than I am an actor, at least that's what my acting teacher told me when we played a few weeks ago at Manhattan Plaza and went out for a drink afterward. This is a city of drinkers. It was not until I moved here in August that I started drinking seriously again. And now, it turns out, doing cocaine.

I sit down on the couch with the Absolut and watch Shawn unwrap my present from Adam.

"Cool paperweight," he says, hefting it in his hand.

"A guy I just met gave me that."

"He must be in love with you."

"Something like that." For a moment, I bend over and rest my head in my hands. "Do you want to eat lunch? I feel weak."

"Oh, God no," he says. He sets the paperweight on the floor and reaches back inside and pulls out my boots, leaving the box in the bag. "Cool boots," he says and sets them by the paper-weight. "Let's just drink." He sits beside me on the couch and takes another swig of vodka. "Sarah, we need to be thin and happy on your birthday."

Shawn does some modeling and is always worried about his weight. He even got me into an Emporio Armani ad once, but all you could see was my foot.

He nudges me with his elbow. "You know how I remembered your birthday?"

I bend over again and say a long *no* into my hands.

"It's three days before mine."

I lift up. "Oh, yeah! Happy birthday, Shawn baby." I move to kiss him, what the hell, on the mouth, but he pulls back, scared, like he thinks I'm finally making my move, and jumps up and turns Madonna back on.

I reach for the Absolut, and as I'm swallowing, there's a knock on the door.

Shawn stops dancing. "Ah," he says, "the Mexicans."

Shawn lets them in, and they are like eighteen years old. One is neat and clean shaven and wearing a black down jacket, while the other's trying to grow a mustache and has on a blue plaid flannel shirt over thermal underwear. Shawn introduces me, and I shake both their hands, and their shakes are real formal like they're politicians. Kenny seems a bit more serious than Carlos and wastes no time doing the deal, while Carlos, the one in the down jacket, asks if I model like Shawn, and I say no, although I think about mentioning that Armani ad, then he asks if I'm an actress, and I lie, saying that I'm a tennis pro.

He nods. "Cool," he says.

"When McEnroe can't find a doubles partner, sometimes he calls me," I say.

He nods. "Cool."

Shawn and Kenny walk over, and Kenny gives me a business card that says WHITE MOUNTAIN DELIVERY. It's thin and flimsy and bright white with a red rose in the center, and below the rose are the names Kenneth and Carlos in thick, cursive black letters, with a cell phone number beside each.

"Thanks a lot," I say and put it in my jacket pocket with Adam's cards. God, I need to have my own cards made up.

Shawn is busy cutting lines on the kitchen counter, and I watch him do three of the six. He steps aside and says, "For you."

I hesitate over, but fuck it. I'm Sarah Blair, and I can be anybody. I take the cut-off straw and lean down, holding back my hair. I feel glamorous snorting coke in New York City. And in the midst of doing my second line, I hear a shutter snap, and Shawn has a camera and is laughing like crazy.

"Jesus," I say, shielding my face with my hands, but I pronounce it *hey-seus,* and Kenny and Carlos laugh.

I grab the camera and take a picture of Shawn doing the last line. Then I take some pictures around the apartment of Shawn posing with Carlos, kissing Carlos's cheek, holding Carlos's bicep, parting Carlos's hair. I try to take one of Kenny while he's talking on his cell phone, but he won't let me at first. Then I put my arm around him and hold the camera out in front of us and he doesn't mind this, moves closer to me, and I take our picture.

"Hey," I tell Kenny when he's off the phone and give him the camera, "take a picture of me in my new boots." I sit on the floor to put them on, but they won't zip up over my jeans. I look at Kenny, and he seems disappointed that it doesn't work out. Shawn shakes his head sympathetically.

"I need a skirt," I say, standing up with my boots still on but unzipped now to the ankles.

Kenny and Carlos nod.

"No, I know," Shawn says, halting me with his hand, and he hurries into the kitchen and comes back with scissors.

"You're not going to make the boots short?" Kenny asks.

Shawn gives a dismissive look and gathers up my jeans at mid-thigh.

"Hey," I say. "I like these."

He pierces the denim with one of the blades. "I know they're nice, Sarah, and that's why they'll make splendid shorts."

"Whatever," I say, and he begins to cut. The blade is cold on my thigh.

"You're a true artist," Carlos says.

Shawn raises his head and smiles, then circles me as he cuts off the other side.

I put my hands on Shawn's shoulders for balance and step out of the boots, and he pulls the jeans off for me, one leg at a time, and it feels like he's undressing me, and I glance at Kenny and Carlos, and I like that they're watching. Shawn starts tugging thread from the ends, making a cool fringe.

Kenny and Carlos nod and almost say in unison, "*Me gusta*. I like it."

I put my hands on my hips and tilt my chin down, so my hair falls over one eye, and Kenny raises the camera to take a picture of me. I'm feeling beautiful and theatrical, and without any forethought, I suddenly grow somber and pensive and say, surprising myself, "'There is color in my life, but I'm not aware of any structure.'" It's a line from a scene in *Six Degrees of Separation* that Shawn and I are doing for class.

Shawn stares vacantly at Kenny and Carlos. "'Cézanne would leave blank spaces in his canvasses if he couldn't account for the brush stroke, give a reason for the color.'"

"'Then I am a collage,'" I say, "'of unaccounted-for brush strokes. I am all random.'"

Shawn and I bow, and Kenny takes a picture of us and as the camera starts to rewind, Shawn announces that because it's my birthday Kenny and Carlos will give us a ride in their town car anywhere we want to go.

"You will?" I ask Kenny.

He shrugs, and Carlos jumps in, says, "*Como no*. Of course."

"Sure," Kenny says.

"So, where do you want to go?" I say to Shawn.

"To get something to eat. I thought you were hungry."

"God, I was. I guess I still am. I haven't eaten all day."

"Well, fuck," Shawn says, "let's go." He pulls on an olive-green ski cap that matches his camouflage shirt and grabs the half-drunk bottle of Absolut lying on the couch.

Kenny helps me put on my purple coat, and I button it as we walk downstairs to Kenny's car, at least he's the driver, and I think about calling shotgun, but Shawn beats me to it, and Carlos and I take the back.

"We got a delivery on Canal Street," Kenny says, looking at me in the rearview mirror, "and after that, we'll take you whatever you want."

Maybe I'm thinking of the place where I was born, I don't know, but I'm suddenly craving catfish from Blue Ribbon, not that they fry it like I'm used to back in Arkansas, but it's almost as good, spicy and sweet with Cajun seasoning. And their fried chicken. Shawn says he loves their oysters. Kenny and Carlos don't know what they want, and I recommend steak, the New York strip or the hanger (Chandler and I had steak there in September on her birthday, just the two of us, like most of our nights out in Manhattan), and Kenny and Carlos say they'll take whatever if I'm buying.

We drive down Second Avenue, then Houston, then Bowery to get to Canal, and it takes awhile because it's Friday evening and rush hour. We stop in front of a fish market, and Kenny and Carlos get out, and then Shawn screams, and I see that on the sidewalk is a squid flopping around in spilled crushed ice. Shawn climbs into the backseat with me, and I lock the doors.

"I hate Chinatown," I say. One time I came down here with this girl from school who wanted to buy a fake Gucci watch, and I got my wallet stolen right out of my purse.

"Me, too," Shawn says. "Do you have any Chapstick?"

I give him my purse, and he starts rifling through it. He hands me my cell phone, then my American Express, and while I call in our order, he takes out my lipstick and puts it on. It's brown so it doesn't look too bad. Then he takes out my brush, a ponytail holder, and a barrette and starts separating my hair and begins to braid one side.

Shawn is gentle with his hands. "If acting or modeling doesn't work out," I say, "you should be a hairdresser."

"I'm not that flaming, am I?"

"Oh, no," I say, and without sarcasm, because he gets this way sometimes, serious about himself. "When we first met, I didn't even know you were gay."

He twists on the ponytail holder at the end of the braid and starts working on the other side. "You know," he says, "this wouldn't be nearly as much fun if I were a woman doing this."

I don't know how to answer, and I'm wondering what I will do if acting doesn't work out for me. I don't know. I turn my cell phone back on and call home to check messages. But I don't have any, and when Kenny and Carlos come back, they are surprised to find Shawn and me in the backseat, both quiet and depressed, and me with two perfectly even braids, though one is held with a barrette.

"Okay," says Kenny, "so where's Blue Ribbon?"

I tell him the cross streets but that I don't know how to get there from here, that I'm confused. He's not, though. Kenny takes a quick right onto Sixth Avenue, then another right onto Spring, then a left onto Sullivan, and we're there in three minutes.

Inside, it's already crowded as hell, but I'm able to get the bartender's attention, and he helps me with my order. I come back to the car with two big sacks, and divvy out the steaks to Kenny and Carlos and the oysters to Shawn and save the catfish and fried chicken for me. Kenny starts driving again, another delivery, and I don't really see how he's going to eat a steak with green beans while driving, but Carlos helps him by cutting up the meat, but even that is pretty hard because we only have plastic knives and forks.

The catfish is really spicy tonight, and I have Kenny stop at a deli, and I run in and get some cash, then buy four big bottles of Evian, one for everyone, why not, and a roll of Certs for after.

I eat fried chicken with my hands, and it's delicious. I'm raving about it so much that Kenny wants a piece, and I have plenty to give, and I give Carlos a piece, too, and even hand them the small cup of honey, so they can dip and get the full effect. Shawn says oysters are enough for him, and he takes a drink of Absolut after each one slides down his throat.

We're up by Times Square when Kenny pulls over and lets Carlos make the delivery alone so that he can finish his steak. We're parked right in front of the Virgin Megastore, in the middle of all the neon lights and action.

"This is the best birthday I've ever had," I say.

Kenny smiles at me in the rearview mirror, and Shawn starts singing "Happy Birthday." He's got a great voice and sings the whole song, and Carlos returns as Shawn is finishing, then the two of them sing it again, and at the end, they clap and Kenny whistles.

"I love New York," I say. And Shawn starts singing "New York, New York," and I get out my cell phone and call Chandler. She says she just tried to call me, at home and on my cell, and that makes me feel good. I tell her how I've been out all day, and where I am, then I get an idea, ask her to hold on, and lay the phone on the seat, and Shawn picks it up and starts singing into it. I grab Kenny's headrest to pull myself closer to him. "Kenny," I say, "how about taking me and my friend Chandler to Maxwell's in Hoboken?"

He shrugs. "Sure. It's not that far."

Man, I'm really starting to love Kenneth. I sit back and grab the phone away from Shawn, and I tell Chandler the good news, no Path train for us, and that we'll pick her up in about thirty minutes, which I guess is about how long it will take to get down to her place on University and Tenth.

I ask Shawn if he wants to go, but he waves me away, says he's tired, but he looks depressed, with his head against the window. I'm relieved really because I'm sure Brinson's show is sold out. Brinson always puts me on the guest list plus one, and I doubt I could get in more than one.

When we reach his apartment, Shawn leans over to hug me but then he kisses me good-bye on the lips, winks, then gives me the last of the Absolut. "Have fun," he says and gets out, waving at Kenny and Carlos.

On the way to Chandler's, nobody speaks, and it feels weird with Shawn not in the car, and I'm wondering what in the world I'm doing here with these two guys, kids really.

Chandler is waiting in front of her building, and she looks great. She's wearing a black-and-brown leopard-print coat that somehow still looks conservative on her. I open the door, and she gets in.

"Nice tinted windows," she says. "What are you guys, drug dealers?"

Kenny and Carlos don't say anything, and I give her my White Mountain Delivery card, and she raises her eyebrows.

"They're all right," I whisper. I fish out a twenty from my purse. "Hey, Carlos," I say, "could I have just a bit more?"

I give him the twenty, and he hands me back a small square packet. I open the foil and show Chandler.

"What do you do?" she says.

I put a little on the tip of my forefinger and bring it to the right side of my nose and sniff it, then she does the same.

"This is insane," she says, but does some more, and I can tell she really likes it. There's not a lot there, and we finish after a few turns, and I'm surprised when I see that we're out of the Holland Tunnel and into New Jersey. I look back and see the skyline of Manhattan. Chandler looks back, too, and the lights in the shadow-box buildings begin to flicker. The view is better from over here.

And I'm surprised that Hoboken is so cute and clean-looking. I expected it to be awful, like it is around La Guardia.

I feel pretty fucking cool getting out of a drug dealer's car at Maxwell's. Maybe it's just the cocaine, but my confidence is high, and so is Chandler's.

"*Gracias* and *adios,* Kenny and Carlos," Chandler says, while I quietly give them kisses on the cheek. "What the hell," Chandler says as we're walking in. "This is fun, baby."

From the bar, we can hear Brinson singing in back with his sad Kansas voice, playing his great-grandfather's banjo, playing a song he played for me the first time I stayed over at his apartment. The song is called "Radio for Heartache," and though I can't see him, I know he looks so real and sings with such expression, haggard and slumping and nearly dancing, as if he's not alone, that I wish I weren't afraid to love him.

The bouncer tells us they're sold out, that it's too packed for us to go in, and I feel great telling him I'm on the list. "Sarah Blair plus one," I say, and he finds my name, marks through it with his pencil, then steps aside to let us by. Chandler starts moving to the front, trying to get closer, but I stay back, look around, and see clusters of girls, young and pretty and hopeful and blonde. And as I follow Chandler toward the stage, I stop and speak to the girls. "He's a great guy," I say, giving out Adam's cards. And they take them, and hold them, and feel their raised lettering. "He's a friend of mine," I say, and, "You'll like him," and, "He's smart and funny," until all the cards are gone.

AND WHEN I SHOULD FEEL SOMETHING

APRIL 1996

Chandler

I call my parents to see how everything is in Arkansas. It's the first nice spring day in New York, and I want to tell my father about jogging through Central Park. My mother answers the phone and sounds different, distracted, and says she'll call me back. I read the paper, watch television, and when my mother calls, she says my father has killed himself.

My mom has arranged for a friend's son to take me to the airport. He lives in New Brunswick, New Jersey, and will be here in an hour. He will buy my ticket, and my mother will reimburse his father.

I'm not ready when he buzzes my apartment, but I let him up anyway and try to finish packing before he gets upstairs. I open the door and see a guy and girl, about my age, twenty-four, and hold my hand out to the guy, trying to be polite, and say, "I'm Chandler." He shakes my hand and says his name, then he introduces his girlfriend, but I don't listen. I apologize for not being ready. They ask if they can help me pack, but I say, "No. Thank you. I'll just be a minute."

They watch me, and they look around. They look at my bedroom, at my bookshelf, at the small kitchen that is part of the living room.

Driving to the airport, there is traffic, and I wish he had taken the tunnel. We don't talk much, except about the traffic. I wish I were in a cab.

At the American Airlines counter, he buys my ticket home. "Twelve hundred dollars to Fort Smith, Arkansas," he says, handing it to me. "I'm glad Dad's the one who's buying it." His girlfriend gives him a look, and I say, "Thank you. I really appreciate everything." I don't want to be indebted to him, but I am. I give him and his girlfriend an awkward hug good-bye.

As I'm waiting in line to board the plane, a woman asks me what time it is. I pause too long. The woman says, "My watch stopped." I tell her two-thirty. Once seated, I cry. I don't want to make a scene. I don't want anyone to ask me what's wrong. I put my book in the pocket of the seat in front of me, then I look for it, thinking I put it in my bag. My face is hot and streaked with tears.

At home, people turn and look at me and whisper. My mother doesn't seem right. She's acting light-headed, in a fluttering way, like she's at a party. "Oh, Chandler," she says when she sees me.

Flowers are everywhere, and my mother tells me that there are some for me by the fireplace. I guess Sarah has heard the news. She sent a huge, flashy bouquet, gladiolas and Easter lilies.

A childhood friend of mine is here, my first boyfriend in the sixth grade, and I motion for him to follow me upstairs. "I'm glad you're here," I tell him.

He says, "New York sure has been good to you. Man, oh man."

"What do you mean?" I ask.

"You look so good," he says. "You look really hot."

In a pleasant way, I say that I'm exhausted and ask him to leave, but I feel angry and lie in bed. Various friends of my mother's poke their heads into my room and try to say something. Mostly, they say, "Oh, Chandler."

That night, after everyone has left, my mom gives me two sleeping pills. She has already taken two herself and is drowsy. She climbs into bed with me and holds my arm and says, "He did this for you and for me. It was an act of love." She runs a hand through my hair. "We'll never have to worry about money again."

The next morning I read a photocopy of my father's suicide letter. The police have the original. It's written only to my mother and says that he loves her and me, but he cannot face financial ruin. He says that his insurance policy will pay a million dollars, and that she can pay the bank the four hundred thousand owed, and that the house will be free and clear with six hundred thousand left over, which should be enough for us to be all right. He says that his body will be in the warehouse and for my mother to call Phil Conti, a friend of my father's who is also a lawyer, and for my mother *You do not go down there.* He says that at his office will be instructions regarding the policy and the will and that Phil Conti will handle everything.

The warehouse used to belong to my grandfather, who made his money from real estate, and it's an enormous place divided into sections that are rented out to various businesses for storage. The clearest memory I have of my grandfather is watching him play the eighteenth hole at Hardscrabble. I'm walking past the golf course toward the tennis courts with my friends, and I tell them, "Watch this. That's my grandfather, but he won't recognize me." I yell over and wave at him, and he looks back at me with no recollection. I laugh and my friends laugh, and we keep walking.

There is an office right as you go into the warehouse, and I keep picturing my father walking in, sitting in a chair, placing the butt of a shotgun on the floor and the barrel in his mouth and pulling the trigger.

The funeral plans have been made, but there is still the matter of picking out a casket. I go down to the cemetery with Phil Conti, and it was his son, I learn now, who drove me to the airport. I have only met Phil Conti a couple of times and don't remember that he's from New York. He tells me about growing up in Brooklyn and ending up in Arkansas because of his wife. We talk about Manhattan, and he says that his mother is in a nursing home in the Village on Hudson Street, close to where I live. Phil Conti has a terrific Brooklyn accent. I love Phil Conti, feel grateful to him, and think I will go visit his mother.

There is a brochure with different caskets at different prices. I'm almost certain that I remember my father saying he wanted to be cremated, but I don't say anything. Phil Conti picks out a mid-priced coffin. The funeral director asks if I want to reserve a plot for myself, so that the Carey family can all be buried together.

"No, thanks," I say.

The funeral director says there's not much space left in the mausoleum, which holds Louis Carey, Marie Carey, Ann Carey, and Don Carey, my father's parents, sister, and brother. "Maybe you would like to start another family area outside by some trees," he says. "Or if you like, you could be cremated, and space would be saved because we could put an urn in the same slot, and that's a lot cheaper."

I ask if they could cremate my father, but he says that it's too late, the mortician is already working on him, and of course, it will be a closed casket. Phil Conti tells the guy that we will stick with what we have, and the mausoleum is fine, and thank you very much.

"God, that was horrible," I say in the car home, and Phil Conti smiles, and I laugh a little.

Later that day, Phil Conti brings over the clothes my father was wearing when he shot himself. He got them from the police station. They are in a brown paper bag—a plaid shirt, tan pants, black socks, Nike tennis shoes, and a Timex watch. They have a certain smell to them. It isn't the smell of blood, or of something rotten. It is the smell of guns, and the smell my father had after he went hunting and was cleaning quail.

My mother reminds me that I must send the airline a copy of the death certificate to get some credit for the twelve-hundred-dollar ticket home. She says, "Phil Conti has been so nice to us, and we must get this taken care of right away." I nod. "And from now on," my mother says, "we're going to be smart about money."

Even though there is a full house with friends and people from the church with casseroles, my mother and I go down to my father's law office. Mom says we should start cleaning it out, but I know what we are really doing is looking for clues. My mom looks through his files. I look in his desk drawers and find his life insurance policy with a highlighted section that confirms it will pay off on a suicide if the policy is held for three years. His policy is twenty years old. He got it when he was thirty-six, after surviving a heart attack. I remember growing up all we ever ate were chicken and fish and skim milk and margarine and wheat germ and cantaloupe. I remember my dad getting heart medicine delivered every week and meditating with a special word that he wouldn't tell anyone, doing whatever he could to stay alive.

The next morning, my mother and I ride to the funeral in the back of a limousine, and she points out to me all the prominent people of the community. She even rolls down the window and waves at some of them. I bow my head and put my hand over my eyes.

"Can you believe all these people are here for Ben?" my mother says. "I don't think he had any idea how many people loved him."

The chapel is packed, and there isn't enough room for everyone. "I hope they all sign the guest book," my mother says. "Oh, I sure hope so, too," I say. My mother gives me a look.

During the service, the minister lists my father's accomplishments, but then focuses on his suicide, before saying that we should not remember his death but his life.

At the cemetery, outside the mausoleum, there is a receiving line with my mother and me shaking hands and thanking everyone for coming. There are people I know and people I don't know and don't want to know. What a performance I'm giving and giving. I meet the mayor. "Thanks for coming," I say. I meet my mother's book-club friends. "Thanks for coming," I say. "Thanks for coming." I meet cousins of my father's whom I've heard of but have never seen, and when I look into their faces and speak, I can see my father and myself, and I want so badly to be back home in Manhattan.

· · ·

In New York at night, in the darkness before sleep, I lie in bed and look through the bedroom door for my father. It seems as likely a place as any he would show up. He could peer around the corner, say good night, or hello, or everything all right? If I squint my eyes, I can see an outline of him in the pajamas, robe, and tennis shoes he wore around the house when I was growing up. He normally wore a suit to work, but he thought that when you were at home and with your family, you should be comfortable.

Several months ago, during Christmas break, when I was home in Arkansas, my father and I played a lot of gin rummy. He would say, "Cut them thin, so Ben can win." It was something he said when I was young and first learning to play cards. Yesterday I heard the word *gin* on television and fell apart. Something like that, and I fall into tears, and another day passes.

On television and in movies, there are always people threatening to kill themselves. There are jokes and storylines about insurance policies not paying off on suicides. I know that they do. I want to scream out that they do. And my friends say, "I wanted to kill myself," and don't realize what they've said. They have no idea what is inside me.

When we talk on the phone, my mother makes me promise that I will not kill myself. My mother says if I won't, then she won't either. My mother says, "Now, let's keep our promise to each other." I agree, but it seems crazy that we would say this at all.

My father is the reason that I'm in New York and in law school, and his money will make it easier for me to stay. But it's hard to go to class. I make myself. I can sit through lectures fine. If I get called on, I say, "I don't know." I spend afternoons wandering around Times Square, among tourists, everyone unsure of where to walk next.

I walk to the Ambassador Theater where *Bring in 'Da Noise, Bring in 'Da Funk* is playing. It stars Savion Glover. I've seen him dance before, when I was twelve years old, on a trip here with my father.

The musical is in previews, and I am able to buy a matinee ticket, a good one in the orchestra, maybe because I'm by myself. I wander back into Times Square and wait for the show to begin.

The theater is old with an orchestra and mezzanine. The ceiling is a gray-blue, and a glass chandelier hangs down. The seats are violet. I'm on the fourth row. The curtain is deep red. The beginning isn't seen but heard. There are taps, and it is dark, and then there is light on the dancer's feet, more taps that grow faster, and then there are other sounds, other feet, other dancers. There are drummers. There is a singer. There is a speaker. And being here so close to the dancer, Savion, I feel a charge, and a current runs through my heart, and I am happy, and I won't let myself look at anyone but him because I don't want my happiness to leave.

Some days I fall into fits of hard crying. My shoulders shake, and I scream and feel out of breath. Then I stop myself, even though I'm alone, because somehow I feel like a fake. I am carrying on this big act of grief, and I feel ashamed for putting on such a show. I know I am sad, but the sadness sometimes reaches an evenness. It isn't always outrage.

The week before my father died, I called home to talk to my mother. My father answered the phone, and I hung up. I felt startled. He never answered the phone. Whenever I was home visiting and the phone would ring, neither of us would answer. It drove my mom crazy, but my father and I would look at each other and smile, coconspirators.

I remembered right when he said "hello" that it was my mother's book-club night, and that she wouldn't be there. I know he would have had fun talking to me, once we started talking, but always, in the beginning of conversations, we didn't know what to say to each other, as if we were anyone else we'd meet in the course of a day.

I want to go back to that phone call. I want to say, "Don't do it. Don't leave me yet. You are more than money." Whatever the words are he needs to hear. I at least want to speak this time.

How did he feel that early morning, walking down the stairs, leaving our house, the house he also grew up in, for the last time? Was he crying? Did he pet our cocker spaniel on the way out like he did every other morning?

· · ·

Savion pushes up on one toe and stays. I don't even know where his other foot is. Normally he's on one toe and the other is tapping around him. What I like most about coming here is seeing the differences in each performance. He dances in front of a bank of mirrors, and this time he is louder, his taps heavier. He does different steps. At the end of the solo, he falls to the floor in exhaustion. A woman from the mezzanine yells, "Oh, Savion." He stands up quickly and looks in her direction and grins.

Savion is changing tap dancing, changing Broadway. He will be remembered. He matters.

When Savion taps he hardly looks at or faces the audience. He wears loose black pants, an old T-shirt. His shoulders slump a little. He is in control when he dances, not only with movement, but with sound, and somehow with emotion. When I'm watching, and hearing the taps, I'm right with him, and I feel like I can do, am doing, what he's doing. We are in this together, and he knows I need him. He must know that.

Seeing the musical is helping me. It is because of Savion that I get out of bed, leave my room, talk to anyone. It is because I know I can see him dance again. I can see him Tuesday night and then again Saturday matinee. He is someone I have come to depend on.

My father used to send me checks in the mail and write, "To cover a few matinees." He would say that if you see a good musical, you walk out feeling like a million bucks. Despite everything, I still like that expression because my father said it.

The tears are light and slow, but they are always near. They come to me now as I'm sitting in the back of a cab, watching out the windows, looking at buildings and people on Sixth Avenue. I am jealous of girls with fathers, of families, of any two people walking together.

I reach into my purse for the picture of my father I carry with me. It was taken when he was twenty-six here in New York at a law-firm party. I hold it in my hand, a beautiful faded color with a white jagged border. My father stands in a circle with the other young associates. He looks strong and handsome and happy to be where he is.

The cab takes me past Macy's and Bryant Park, moving closer to the familiar turn on West Forty-ninth Street. I put the picture back in my purse, and I don't feel as sad because I know he was good, and was alive, and was my father.

People say I am like my father. I am smart and kind. I am a good tennis player. I am nice looking. I also like staying home. I like to wear pajamas any time of the day.

When I go to see Savion, I prefer to go alone. When I went once with friends, they said, "Oh, it was good. Have you seen this other play? It's good, too." Even Sarah wasn't visibly moved, and I felt lost that even she could not understand that what we were witnessing was amazing.

The cab drops me at Forty-ninth and Broadway, and I walk the half block west to the Ambassador. I always get a thrill walking this small stretch, seeing others dressed up, rushing to the same theater. I'm not alone at all, and I don't have to speak or shake a hand.

My seat is on the third-row center, four from the aisle. There is no one yet next to me, and I begin to feel awkward and obvious. It is not until the lights dim and the orchestra begins playing that the usher leads several people down the aisle. Even in the dark, the whole audience sees who they are. A bodyguard, a beautiful woman, and a movie star. And the movie star sits right beside me. I have seen him before, but I don't know his name, but those around me do, and they whisper. At first, I have to make myself not look at the movie star, but then I get caught up in Savion's dancing.

During intermission everyone wants the movie star's autograph, and I feel almost sorry for him. He doesn't know how to respond. To get away from the crowd, I think, he turns to me and asks how I like the show. I say with all the enthusiasm I've ever spoken with that the dancer is the greatest tap dancer in the world, and this play is better than any book I've read or film I've seen.

"Yes, yes," he says.

We are looking at each other and nodding. I say, "I've seen it five times." I hate to say I've seen it more.

"This is my second time," he says.

I smile.

"It's fantastic," he says.

"It's the only thing that makes me feel better," I say.

"Yeah," he says. "Yeah."

On my first trip to New York, my dad had gotten two rooms at the Waldorf that were connected, so I could have my own room. I was only twelve. At night, I would sit in front of the window in my pajamas and lean against the glass, and listen to the cars, the sirens, the subway, people talking and laughing, the doorman whistling for a taxi. My parents would watch me and say, "What are you doing?" and I'd answer, "Listening."

We had already seen *Big River* and *Biloxi Blues,* and for our last night, we had tickets to *Cats.* I did not want to see *Cats* no matter how much my mother did or how often she told me they were T. S. Eliot's cat poems. I wanted to see *The Tap Dance Kid* with Savion Glover. I had seen an ad for it, and at the time, I was a Michael Jackson freak, and Savion reminded me of Michael as a kid. Savion was about my age and on Broadway, and I wanted to see him. My dad, without too much persuasion, gave up our *Cats* tickets and bought three tickets for *The Tap Dance Kid.* He even got a limousine to take us to the play. Our driver was named Mannie, and I kept his company card on my bulletin board at home for a long time after.

I remember we were three of the very few white people in the audience. The kid on stage was smiling and playing music with his feet. All the dancers had on tuxedos, which I thought was nice. I kept nudging my parents, saying, "Did you see that?" and "This is incredible." They would smile and look at each other. My father was wearing wire-rimmed glasses, and they moved a little as he smiled and nodded in agreement with me. I knew he didn't like it the way I did, but I let him know that I loved it, and that was all he needed.

After the show, I bought three *Tap Dance Kid* sweatshirts. At school, I wore one and gave the other two to friends. There was the proof all over the school that I had been to New York City.

• • •

I moved to New York two years ago for law school at NYU. I had no money to come here, and my father didn't have it to give to me.

We all sat in the den to discuss my going to school. My father put on his glasses. "I can't take care of my family," he said.

"Everyone takes out loans," I said.

He sat with a legal pad in his lap, writing down figures, adding what he could afford to pay. "I have these two cases," he said. "One of them has to pay big."

The two cases involved personal injury. He was not used to that type of work, waiting for a settlement or a judgment before he could get paid. He was used to billing hours to a corporation and getting paid each month.

When he finally admitted that his law practice was failing and that we were running out of money, my mother found him these cases. The plaintiffs were two of her acquaintances who quickly became good friends. My father didn't have the money or experience to try the cases, so he got the help of a personal injury firm in St. Louis. He felt if they were willing to put up millions of dollars on behalf of his cases, he was sure to win. My father felt his luck was changing. He felt like the cases just fell in his lap.

My mother was sitting next to me, and she said in a pleading voice, "What will we do if they don't? How are we going to live?"

My father's eyes narrowed, and he shook his head. "Don't say that. I can't stand it when you say that."

"How did this happen to us?" my mother said.

I didn't understand that either. We were rich when I was young. My father was a corporate lawyer. When he was in his twenties, he had worked for a prestigious firm on Wall Street. In Arkansas, he'd worked for the same corporation for twenty years. When it was taken over, he lost his only client. He had one interview to work with a firm in New Orleans, and when he didn't get the job, that was it. He didn't send his résumé out again. He told us that he didn't want to move, that he would figure things out. "I can get clients. I don't mind doing wills and divorces. Not to worry," he said. "I'm a winner. Everything will be fine." So for years, my mother and I thought everything was fine.

My mother, who had always lived in Arkansas, said, "I blame you for her wanting to go to New York City. It is all your fault."

At that, my father looked at me and smiled, and I knew we were in this together, and I would be able to go.

• • •

I love the freedom of New York. I can walk around, and no one knows me. No one knows or cares what has happened to me. I can't imagine how my mother is making it back in Arkansas, how she's able to go to the grocery store or the bank, where she is certain to see someone who knows. I feel so lucky to live in Manhattan, and sometimes I even say out loud to my father, "Thank you." Then I feel ashamed. I only think about myself, about being a daughter who has lost her father, not about my mother and what she has lost.

I decide to call and apologize and ask how *she* is, but when my mother answers, I don't say anything and hang up.

Back in the fall, months before my father died, I walked to

the Public Theater hoping to see Savion dance. I already knew the musical was sold out. When I had called earlier about a ticket, a woman told me the show was moving to Broadway, and I could see it in April. I walked down to the Public anyway. I wasn't sure why. I knew I didn't have a chance of getting in. And then I saw Savion. He was leaning against the outside brick of the theater, staring out into the street and the sky, smoking a cigarette. I looked at him as if he were a painting, something to be studied. The white of his shirt, his dark hair compared to his lighter skin, his black pants, and his shoes.

I like Times Square. I like the bright lights of the electric signs. I don't mind walking past Peepland or Runway 69. To me, the neon Xs from strip clubs and the yellow arches from McDonald's somehow add to the beauty. My mother was always afraid of walking through Times Square and I was, too, when I first moved here. And it probably isn't entirely smart now, walking around without reason, away from Times Square and into Hell's Kitchen, as day turns to night. But since my father died, I don't feel like anyone can hurt me.

Without intention, I walk down Forty-ninth, past Broadway, to the Ambassador. A scalper sees me, walks up to me like he knows me, and offers a ticket. I reach into my purse and pay him. I walk to the side door, the one with fewer people, only one ticket taker, and pray the ticket is not fake. Then, at once, I feel someone brush against me, and I look back and see the white T-shirt, and I look up and see the hair, almost in dreads, and I am at his shoulders, and he passes me, and I'm not sure I am appreciating the good fortune of brushing next to the dancer, this man who I believe is saving me.

I don't feel nervous or excited. I don't want to talk to him. I don't feel anything. And when I should feel something, some kind of gratitude, it is too late, and my chance to feel what I should have felt has passed.

After seeing the musical as many times as I have, I want to skip through certain parts. My mind wanders during the songs and the words. Only when the dancer who brushed against me is dancing, is my mind where I wish it to be. Only when he is making music with his tap, notes I have never heard, as if he is inventing them at every performance.

What I feel is the smooth slide, tap, scrape, tap, tap, tap, scrape, and I remember looking up at the dancer, and his face is serious and almost sad, tired, not different from mine.

Floating

Leigh

After two days of rain, I'm finally feeling the sun on my face and arms and feet for the first time this summer, and it's the last day of my vacation. I'm lying on my new blue raft and wearing my new yellow one-piece. The water is cold but not too cold as I turn myself around with my hands and float lazily back toward the other side of our pool. I'm the only one out here in the entire apartment building, so it's easy to dream, to place myself where I wish I were. In a swimming pool facing the ocean. In Florida, in Destin, and by myself. Far from Fort Smith, Arkansas, and this married life. And the pool in Destin, Florida, is like this one, small and clean and unshaded and shaped like an eight.

Next door to Andre's, where I work as the assistant manager, there is a travel agency, and sometimes on my break, I browse through their brochures on Cancún and Hawaii and the Bahamas, but Florida, especially Destin, still looks the best to me, with long white beaches and aqua-green water. And it's within reach. It's possible. I've never been farther than Dallas and Tulsa, and no more eastward than Little Rock. I can't imagine what a fifteen-hour drive would feel like.

The sky is cloudless, a pale blue except for a plane crossing and leaving a trail of white. I'm following its path when I hear someone unlatch the gate to the pool. I look over and see my husband, Cassidy, coming toward me, dressed for work at Movieland, in tennis shoes, jeans, and a T-shirt. And my God, his head is shaved.

"Hey, what do you think?" he says. "Do I look like a rock star?"

"Yeah, like a rock star living in Fort Smith," I say.

He drags a deck chair to the edge of the shallow end and sits down and grins. I paddle closer to him, and he leans low enough for me to run my hand over the rough, shaved hair.

"It feels a little funny," I say. "But you look pretty good."

"It's liberating," he says. "Hell, I don't care if I start to lose my hair now."

I smile. We haven't actually had this much of a conversation in a long time. For the past week, Cassidy's gone straight from Movieland to rehearsal, playing rhythm guitar for some new band, and he's come home about two in the morning when I was sound asleep.

"I wanted to tell you," Cassidy says, "that I saw Mrs. Carey yesterday afternoon."

"You did?" I say.

"Well, when she came in, I didn't recognize her, you know, I just wasn't thinking, and when she was checking out I asked what name the account was under, and when she answered, when she said, 'Ben Carey,' she started crying. And do you know what she was renting, Leigh? *The Untouchables* and *Zulu*."

He shakes his shaved head, like Mr. Carey was awful for committing suicide and Mrs. Carey is pitiful for wanting to rent two of his favorite movies. I loved Mr. Carey. I feel like I knew him better than I ever even knew Chandler. The night in the freezing rain and snow, when Mr. Carey helped me with my car and bought me dinner at Wendy's, we talked so easily that anyone could have mistaken us for daughter and father. I don't need to meet my own father to know with certainty that he would be nothing like how Mr. Carey was that night or any other time he's ever nodded or said hello.

"Well, did you talk to her?" I say.

"I couldn't," he says. "She could tell I knew what happened. Then she paid, and I gave her the receipt and movies, and we just looked at each other. It was kind of spooky."

"You should have said something." I shut my eyes and paddle away.

"What?" he says. "Why are you mad at me?"

But I don't answer. It's sunset, and I'm walking down the beach in Destin. Seagulls float above the waves. Pelicans crash into the water.

"Whatever," says Cassidy, and I hear footsteps, then the gate opens and clicks shut.

Cassidy and I have only been married three months. After six years of dating, we got married at the courthouse the day after he proposed, on Valentine's Day. That night for our honeymoon we stayed at the Holiday Inn City Center, which is the nicest hotel in Fort Smith—there's a piano in the lobby and an atrium with a waterfall that cascades five stories. And at the time, that seemed enough, because Cassidy was a nice guy, the only person I'd ever slept with, and I loved him. I still love him. He's been as good to me as anyone can be who refuses to live anywhere but here.

Cassidy proposed the same day Mr. Carey helped me with my car. Mr Carey and I talked about Chandler and two big court cases, and just before he was about to leave, I told him about Cassidy's proposal, and he seemed so pleased and happy for me, so proud, that when I spoke to Cassidy when I got home, I accepted.

I was at Andre's taking orders, chicken lasagnas and fancy soups to be sent to the Carey house, when I found out that Mr. Carey died, had killed himself, that kind man, with a shotgun.

The manager told me that she expected more of these orders, foods to soothe, she called them, and we should let them pile up before our delivery guy carried them over.

I started crying at work, and I couldn't control my crying, or keep my shoulders from shaking. I felt like such a fake, and I hoped I wasn't crying harder than Chandler or Mrs. Carey. It didn't feel right crying so hard. Andre's let me go home early and let me off the next day to go to the funeral, and I tried to go. It was a bright spring day, but still cool, and I wore a gray silk blouse under a black jumper and drove to the Methodist church and parked my car in the lot and sat there watching others go in. There were so many people, dressed up, like it was Sunday, and not a Tuesday morning. I watched a limousine pull up, and Chandler and Mrs. Carey got out, and Chandler looked exactly the same, just how she looked in high school, with shoulder-length blonde hair, and she had on a black jumper like mine but with a pale pink blouse underneath. I expected her to look different, with a sharp edge, like how New York people look on television, and because she didn't, that made it easier for me to get out of my car and walk inside the church and follow others to the chapel to speak to her.

But the chapel was too crowded to get in. A lot of us couldn't get in. Some were signing a guest book, and I wanted to do that, too, but there was a line, and I started crying in that hard way, and people I didn't know turned to look at me, and I turned away and walked back to my car and drove to my mother's. She was home and still wearing one of her big T-shirts she sleeps in, because she had a late night waitressing at Chili's. And when I saw her I started crying again, and she held me for a long time, right there at the open front door. She acted, for once, just like a mother is supposed to act, how I imagine Mrs. Carey has always acted with Chandler.

I hate to think of Mrs. Carey sitting home right now watching *Zulu* and *The Untouchables,* all those grisly deaths. It's been a month since Mr. Carey died, and I haven't even gone over there to see her and take a gift of some kind. And I want to tell her about that night with Mr. Carey. And if I don't do it today, tomorrow I'll be back to work, and months will pass.

I stretch for the ladder and heave myself out of the pool, then lean over the edge for my raft and shake it off. I don't give myself time to talk myself out of going. I don't stop to dry off, I just grab my towel and pat my face and neck as I'm walking past the gate and around the courtyard to my apartment.

I'm barely wet anyway, so I throw on shorts and a purple Polo T-shirt over my bathing suit and slip on a pair of sandals, then try to decide what I should take. I thought while I was on vacation that Cassidy and I would find the time together to try the gourmet foods that I've been sneaking home from work, but most of it is still unopened. So I get one of the nice Andre's sacks that I keep plenty of in the kitchen pantry. They're made of thick, glossy paper and are coated with wax on the inside, and on the outside, they're a forest-green color, with ANDRE'S in gold lettering.

I open up the cabinets and look in the refrigerator, and this is what I grab to put in the sack—a jar of Manzanillo Olives with Lemon and Thyme, a jar of Hot Pepper Jelly, a bag of freshly ground Banana-Nut Coffee, a box of Carr's Table Water Crackers, and a block of Cheddar-Feta Cheese. I remove the price tags and wrap each item in green tissue paper the way I would at work.

In the car, I start getting scared and begin to slow down below the limit once I turn onto Greenwood Avenue, where Mrs. Carey lives. People new to grief always scare me. Though I'm used to sadness, I've never known the kind of grief that Chandler and Mrs. Carey must know now. So I try to calm myself by thinking of Florida, the hypnotic sound of waves and the sight of sand darkening and whitening as the surf washes back and forth, but it's calming for only a moment because the white sand soon reminds me of snow. And how the snow was beginning to fall and gather like white caps on the frozen ground back in February, just as Mr. Carey and I were leaving Wendy's to drive over to Exxon for the wrecker. It's difficult for me to imagine how a man who would point into the sky and marvel at snow could kill himself.

There are those around town, sometimes customers, who talk about it like they're discussing a soap opera and not real people who live among us. "Hey, have you heard about that lawyer who shot himself?" someone might say in Andre's. "Can you believe he'd be that selfish? To leave his family destitute?" And they shake their heads and bring their food to the counter for checkout, and I, needing my job, say nothing in return, nothing I want to say, like *You're wrong. Mr. Carey would not leave them destitute. He is generous and good.* But I say nothing more than "Thank you. Please come again."

I've never been to this house of the Careys, and I drive by, trying to tell if anyone's home. The house I spent the night in with Chandler was much different, rock and wood and modern-looking. Where they live now is classic—green and white with three tall pillars in front, white rocking chairs on the porch. I circle the block before pulling into the driveway.

I take several slow breaths, wishing I had a cigarette, but telling myself not to think of cigarettes again, that I'm not going back to them, that I need to breathe and go and just do it, and I grab the Andre's sack and walk to the front door and ring the bell. I wait a moment, and I'm feeling so nervous and afraid, but I want to do this. This is something I have to do.

I don't hear anything inside, so I look through the front windows, through slats of thick wooden blinds to see if Mrs. Carey's home, but it's hard to see from the glare of the sun. I walk the length of the porch to where the sun is not as bright and look through more windows. This room looks empty, but fancy, with rose-colored walls and hardwood floors, antique couches, marble tables, a grandfather clock, a gold-framed mirror over the fireplace. I press my ear to the window, and I hear the grandfather clock ticking.

I walk back to the driveway, and I notice a dogwood blooming in the front yard, jonquils and pansies planted in the flower bed. The yard looks so neat and kept up. It looks like a house where happy people would live, gardening in wide-brim hats in the afternoons. My mother, with her hair up in a bandanna, will cut the grass, but that's it. The grass doesn't get raked or edged, and she's let the flower beds along the front of her duplex become overgrown with weeds and sprouting trees.

I set the Andre's sack on the pavement and stand on my toes, bracing myself with my hands, to peek into the garage windows, and I see Mr. Carey's blue Blazer and Mrs. Carey's Oldsmobile.

"Hello," I hear Mrs. Carey say behind me, "can I help you?"

I come down off my toes and ease myself around and smile awkwardly at her. But she's not mad or suspicious looking. I can tell she's been out for a walk because she's sweating a little in her blue cotton dress with tennis shoes, and she just wants to know how she can help me.

"Mrs. Carey," I say.

"Oh, Leigh," she says, and her voice breaks as she says my name.

I pick up the Andre's sack and hand it to her. "I wanted to give you something."

"Thank you," she says. She opens the sack and looks in, unwrapping the coffee, then something else, and then stops. "How sweet," she says and leans forward and hugs me. "Would you like to come inside? Come inside, Leigh."

"Okay," I say. I follow her through the back gate up a flagstone sidewalk, past a blonde cocker spaniel sleeping under a wrought-iron table.

"That's Jesse," she says, "short for Jessica," and the dog lifts her head a moment but stays where she is. "She's a *little* over-weight. That's what Sarah Blair said one time. You know how everyone in her family is so skinny and healthy."

We walk through the utility room into the kitchen. Mrs. Carey fixes us some iced tea, and I look at the pictures hanging on the wall behind the kitchen table. There is a school picture of Chandler I recognize from junior high, one that she also gave me. There is one of just the back of Mr. Carey in a red shirt swinging a golf club, with green valleys and mountains in the background. I touch the frame with my finger.

Mrs. Carey sees me and says, "That was taken at Sewanee, where Chandler went to school. And Ben."

It feels strange hearing Mr. Carey called by his first name.

"When Ben was in college there, he played on the golf team. He was really reminiscing that day to Chandler and me as we went with him in the golf cart." She laughs. "Chandler drove, of course."

She sits down at the table with two glasses of iced tea, then I sit down, and we both take a drink.

"This is the house Ben grew up in," Mrs. Carey says. "I think he was the happiest here."

"I'm sure sorry about everything, Mrs. Carey. I really liked Mr. Carey."

"And he liked you, too, Leigh," she says and begins to cry but stops herself. "He told me about taking you to get a tow truck. About how pretty you were and how fun it was to talk to you. How you reminded him of Chandler out in the snow."

"He did?" I say.

"Oh, yes, and, Leigh, that is the ultimate compliment from Ben. He never said too much about anyone, except maybe Chandler or Jesse out there."

I smile, then worry I'm smiling too much. "And he talked about *you*," I say.

"He did?" she says.

"Yeah, about you getting mad at him for all the bowls he would use at lunchtime."

She laughs. "Not only that, Leigh. Just before he killed himself, he would use two napkins at every meal."

I feel startled but try not to show it and keep talking. "And he talked about you and him taking Chandler to speech therapy. About how y'all practiced every night with cards for months until she was finally able to say *yellow* and *lawyer.*"

She makes a face like she might scream from laughter, then I realize she's angry, hysterical. "Leigh," she says, her face now flushed red, "I am so mad at him. Not just for what he did to me but for what he did to Chandler."

"Why did he do it?" I say, and I clear my throat because I'm speaking in a whisper. "Did he lose those cases he was working on?"

"No," she says, her anger passing, "they're still going on. But I doubt we're going to win them. He didn't think we were going to win them."

I nod and sip my tea and wonder if they are destitute, but I don't want to ask that.

She raises her eyebrows, and I see there is no white to the whites of her eyes, she's been crying so long. "He did it over money, Leigh. He thought he was worth more to us dead than alive."

"What do you mean?" I say.

"He had a big insurance policy, and he'd had it for so long that it paid off on suicide, and now Chandler and I have more money than we really want."

She covers her face with her hands and starts crying, and I get up and walk around the table and hold her shoulders.

"Mrs. Carey, I don't know my father. I've never even seen

him." But what I'm trying to say doesn't sound appropriate. That Chandler is lucky to have had many years with a father that I never had, and from now on she will have to live like I live, and that is sad, and that is permanent. And nothing she can ever do, no one she can ever love, will ever change that.

Mrs. Carey lowers her hands from her face. "Ben and I were set up for our first date." She smiles, but tears still stream from her eyes. "I thought he was the cutest thing I'd ever seen. He'd just moved back from New York, and I hadn't lived anywhere but Arkansas, and he would talk about eating oysters in Manhattan. *Man*hattan, he'd say. I just couldn't believe that he liked me, too."

"He told me about the oysters," I say, "and the good bread everywhere." I pat her back. "He said he hoped Chandler was eating some of that good bread."

She stops crying and laughs. "Oh, Leigh," she says. "Thank you for coming over."

"He told me, too, about all that crazy food he would eat for lunch."

She laughs more and leads me to the pantry to show me cans of sardines and beets and sauerkraut and spinach. "I don't think I'll ever be able to throw these away," she says.

"Then don't," I say.

She smiles. "This is the first time I've been able to talk about Ben and really laugh. Thanks for coming over here, Leigh."

"It was great to see *you* again, Mrs. Carey. You'll have to drop by Andre's some time."

"I will," she says, and we hug each other.

I leave the same way I came in, through the utility room, and I turn back once and watch the outline of Mrs. Carey through the screen door. She's bent over, taking clothes from the dryer and putting them in a basket.

On my way out, I pet the cocker spaniel. "You're not too fat," I say.

In the car going home, I feel so brave to have left my raft to see Mrs. Carey and gone inside with her to remember Mr. Carey that I think about driving all the way to Destin to find an apartment of my own on the beach. White sand. Seagulls floating above the waves. Pelicans crashing into the aqua-green water. But there are things to say to Cassidy yet. Things to work out. Or try to work out. More bravery needed. And I decide I will never leave him or anyone wondering what has happened to me and why.

FLORENCE IN A ROOM

JUNE 1996

Sarah

So I haven't been out of my room for four days. It's a really nice room, and it's not like I haven't been to Florence before. I came here when I was in high school, and I've been to the museums, all through the Uffizi and the Bargello, and I've been to the churches, for hours in Santa Croce and the Duomo, so I know what it's all about. But I've never stayed in the Grand Hotel Villa Cora on Viale Machiavelli, which has to be the most beautiful street in the world. I can see the Duomo and some other monuments that I don't know the names of, and all these wonderful trees and hills and houses with terra-cotta roofs in this panoramic view from my window, and from another window, I have a view of the Villa Cora pool, with bright blue water surrounded by red geraniums, maybe begonias, and manicured shrubs and marble statues. To get to this place, we were driven through the center of the city, and it was crowded and just plain dirty, so I know that Florence looks much better from up here.

I'm watching my family out by the pool, and I'm wearing a thick Villa Cora bathrobe, which has become my standard Italian outfit. My dad, C. H., is lying on a deck chair dressed in beige linen pants and a bright pink shirt, a departure, and next to him is his live-in girlfriend, I'm sure soon-to-be sixth wife, Destiny. She's at least close to his age, forty to his fifty-four, and wearing a loose olive-green sundress and, of course, her crystal necklace. She's all into New Age. Her daughter, Rain, is sitting at the bar with my younger half-sister, Whitney, and they are both wearing faded Levi's and black T-shirts, with matching woven friendship bracelets. They're still into the Grateful Dead. My half-brother Paul and his girlfriend are actually in the pool, even though it's early June and almost evening, and I'm sure the water is cold. From up here, everybody down there looks alike, thin with dark hair. Up here, I'm thin, too, but my hair is blonde. I just had it done in New York, the day before I flew in.

I feel like such an outcast, how I look, what I'm all about. Everyone in my family discusses movies and plays they've seen at length like they're experts. There's this quote by Uta Hagen, who's this great actor and teacher and whose book we're using in class, that says, "The lack of respect for acting seems to spring from the fact that every layman considers himself a valid critic." What a bunch of laymen down there.

Chandler sounded so surprised and happy when I called yesterday. I told her how C. H. got us all these rooms and how everyone is paired up and how I'm the only one in a room by myself and that I needed her here in Florence as much as she needed to get away from New York. It's been two months since her father killed himself, and all she's been doing is going to this same musical to see this tap dancer, Savion Glover. Thank God she'll be here tomorrow.

There's a knock on the door, and I grab 5,000 lire from the stack of 5,000-lire notes I have on the dresser for tip money. The last two nights I've been adventurous, ordering loin of rabbit stuffed with porcini mushrooms and zucchini, then stingray and a mixed salad with yogurt mayonnaise and chives, but tonight it's penne pasta and cream of pea soup.

I love opening the door to see the room-service guy standing there in his burgundy jacket and black bow tie, with my tray of food, under silver cover, balanced on one hand. *"Ciao,"* I say and step back and point to the bed, and he sets the tray down, and I'm glad to see he didn't forget my bowl of ice.

"Grazie," I say and hand him his tip.

"Prego," he says.

I love speaking Italian.

I turn on the television and try again to find the French Open. I watched it all day yesterday, but today I've had no luck finding it. Just game shows I don't understand, real chatty and sexual, with *The Price Is Right*–type girls who don't seem to model anything but themselves, and a lot of long infomercials about high-tech cellulite-removal systems. I give up on tennis and stop on Sky News, then refill my glass with ice and make another vodka tonic from the mini-bar. I'm glad the mini-bar woman comes in each afternoon to restock. I don't get drunk ever, but it's fun to begin in the morning and float along at a steady pace until I've taken my bath and gone back to sleep.

I get in bed under the covers and sit cross-legged and spread out my napkin, which is mint green and has the hotel's insignia on it, like everything in this room, the bath towels, the pillow cases, the shoe mitt, the silverware. I tear a roll in half and butter it, then unveil the soup and pasta and begin to eat, going back and forth between the spoon and the fork, until I'm tired of eating and watching the news and decide to go back to drinking. I start my bath, then make two vodka tonics to take with me.

As I ease into the hot water, I think about how close I've come to committing suicide. When I was fifteen, I wanted to overdose on Xanax when I saw my boyfriend dead after he wrecked his car because he was leaning out the window waving at me. And in my first year of college, I lived in the dorm on a high floor and had an overwhelming urge to jump out of a window for no apparent reason. Sometimes when I'm acting I have to summon those feelings before I can rage or cry or look sad enough to cry, but I've never been able to make any sense of them. I have a teacher who tells us that we need to protect our pain, that to understand it too much would only weaken it and rob us of the magic that can make us great.

Chandler's father was such a nice, manly kind of man, funny at times, in a clever, quiet way, yet a sensitive man, and that always means a sort of sad one. I tend to like sad people.

My friend Adam who's an investment banker just last week started working at Morgan Stanley in Times Square, and he says his office looks out onto a billboard with a giant blonde model in lacy red underwear. He jokes that this is the closest relationship he's ever had with a woman, then he gets despondent, saying it's really hard to concentrate there and that it's impossible to find someone in the city.

My boyfriend, Brinson Carr, who has never told me he loves me or anything, is still writing and singing sad songs, and because he's on this solo tour for the summer, we probably won't talk again until we're both back in New York.

I drink the last of the second vodka tonic, then drain out the bath water, stand up, and turn on the shower to shampoo and condition my hair. Then once I've dried off and wrapped the towel around my head, I put on my conservative white pajamas I bought for the trip. I'm brushing my teeth when someone knocks.

God, I wonder which family member it could be.

"Who is it?" I say.

"Your brother Paul."

I open the door, and he's got his arms crossed like he's scolding me, but he's smiling, too.

"Hello, Sarah," he says. "Having a good time?"

"A great time."

He nods, then points a thumb down the hall. "We're all going into town to a pizzeria, then to Meccano. It's supposed to be a cool club. Rain and Whitney went last night."

121

"I've already eaten," I say. "And I hate clubs."

"Oh, that's right, you like dark grungy dives with sad singers from Kansas."

"That's right." I take the towel off my head and shake my hair so water spots his shirt. "I feel comfortable there and in ritzy elegant places like here. But thanks for asking, though, Paul."

"No, thank *you,* sis," he says, brushing his shirt with the back of his hand.

"I'd be careful with your girlfriend," I say. "I think I saw the pool boy eyeing her today."

"You did?" he says.

"Yeah, and Whitney and Rain and Destiny," I say.

"Well, don't fall out the window watching us have all the fun." He winks at me like he always does when he has a new girlfriend and is feeling smug. He starts to walk away. "Maybe when Chandler gets here you'll want to go out."

"Maybe, baby," I say.

"After 'while, crocodile," he says and dances down the hall like a crazy disco person.

I turn around and push the door closed with my foot, then shift my hips, then sling my wet hair around, then begin punching the air, the way I would dance if I were at Meccano.

• • •

I've been awake for an hour watching CNN World News, mainly about the weather in Africa, when the room-service guy finally knocks with my breakfast. I go to the dresser to get 5,000 lire, then open the door to let him in. He's been here before and knows to set the tray and the *Herald Tribune* on the bed. I hand him his tip and climb back under the covers, and instead of leaving, he starts opening curtains, then windows, then shutters, and sunlight pours in, and I'm afraid the mosquitoes are going to be next.

"Hey," I say.

"Prego," he says and smiles and walks out.

I get up and close the windows. Last night I didn't get one of the windows closed all the way, and a mosquito came in and buzzed in my ear, and it sounded as big as a boat. I tried to find it for a while, then decided to get some toilet paper and wad it into my ears, so the mosquito couldn't get inside my canals and I could go back to sleep. Then when I woke up this morning I had two bites on my neck, and I saw that mosquito just resting itself on the wall above the headboard, on the fresco of the verbena arbor, with the flowers that hang down like bunches of grapes from a trellis, and it must have thought it was back home in the real verbena arbor out by the pool. It was bigger than any mosquito I ever saw growing up in Arkansas. But it's dead now.

So I unveil my food, and voila, it's exactly what I ordered last night when I filled out my breakfast card and hung it on the door. Ham, scrambled eggs, a fruit plate of diced cantaloupe, pineapple, bananas, and strawberries, then of course I have my bowl of ice and a glass of orange juice and a basket of croissants and hard tasteless rolls, with butter and jelly and Nutella. I've really grown to like Nutella in the morning, that exquisite blend of hazelnuts and chocolate.

After eating maybe half of everything, but all of the Nutella, I put the tray in the hall outside my door and decide I better start getting ready for Chandler. She's supposed to arrive around eleven, so I only have a couple of hours.

I begin by tweezing my eyebrows, which I'm not very good at, but I try my best to give them a slight arch. In the bathtub, I shave under my arms and at my bikini line, in case I ever do go out to the pool, and work my way down my legs, even getting my big toes. I don't feel like standing to do my hair, so I take the shower head off its hook and shampoo and condition, then get up and rinse everywhere before stepping out. I dry myself with one of the thick Villa Cora towels, then rub on this great-smelling Villa Cora lotion, then put on my Villa Cora bathrobe and go to the mini-bar and open a small bottle of champagne and look out the window at the salmon-colored dome of the Duomo.

I haven't seen Chandler much lately, not because I haven't tried. In New York, I would call her close to every day, and we went out a few times, but most of the time she would say she just couldn't go out and be around people. And I'd tell her I understood that. But I want her to have fun here. I want her stay at the Grand Hotel Villa Cora to be a real vacation, one where she'll actually vacate her life and become something else.

I finish my glass of champagne while the maid is here. Normally I just take clean towels at the door, but I want the room to look nice for Chandler. When the maid is finished with everything, I give her 5,000 lire and go back to the bathroom to dry my hair. The dryer doesn't have a lot of power or heat, but I have the time. Then I apply foundation, blush, eyeliner, pink eyeshadow, this shiny blue mascara that looks good with my blue eyes. I'm like a whole new person, and I slip on a bright pink silk skirt and matching top and nude snakeskin heels, looking real Italian, and I sort of waltz over to the mini-bar as I imagine Eugenia the Empress must have waltzed here or in some other room of this hotel when this place was her own private residence following the death of her husband, Napoleon III. I pour another glass of champagne, then saunter to the window facing the pool to see if Paul and C. H. and everyone are there.

But I only see Paul on his raft and the pool boy, who's not really a boy but a man with a full-time job and is always wearing a tiny black Speedo and is now swimming free-style laps past Paul. I push open the window and whistle two notes, the first one higher than the second, Paul's old signal when we were living together in college that he was home, but he doesn't hear me, so I whistle again, louder this time, and he lifts his head, shielding his eyes from the sun, and whistles back.

"How's the water?" I yell.

Paul flips off his raft and swims underwater, under the pool boy, to the ladder and climbs out. Then the pool boy speeds up his stroke and races up the steps at the shallow end and grabs one of the blue towels stacked on a table by the bar, and Paul stands there dripping wet, doesn't move an inch, until the pool boy hands him the towel. Paul pats his face, then hangs the towel around his neck as he walks onto the lawn closer to me.

"What'd you say, Sarah?"

"I said, 'How's the water?'"

"Well, hell," he says, throwing up his arms, "what do you care?"

"I was wondering if it was cold."

"Lord, Sarah," he says and walks back to the pool.

I close the shutters and step away from the window to the mini-bar to make a vodka tonic with the last of the ice that's floating in the bowl.

●   ●   ●

It's almost three in the afternoon when the phone rings and wakes me up from a nap. It's one of the reception guys telling me that Chandler Carey is downstairs, and I tell him to send her up. I go to the armoire and straighten my hair in the mirror. I hope she doesn't cry when I see her. I'm afraid she'll be tired from the long trip and will be even more emotional.

I open the door to see her walking down the hall with a carry-on bag and a backpack and a purse, and she looks excited and happy, with even blonder hair than mine.

I rush out to hug her, and she's still okay, doesn't cry, and I grab her bag, and it's heavy, and she follows me into the room.

"This is incredible," she says and wanders around, then stares out the window with the view of the trees and hills and city in the distance.

"I know," I say and move to stand beside her, then I start crying.

"Don't cry," she says and smiles. "I've got something for you." She sits on the bed and unzips her backpack and pulls out five limes. "For your vodka tonics and my gin and tonics."

"Where did you get those?"

"From the trees right outside along the driveway. Didn't you see them?"

I shake my head. "I don't remember."

"Do you care if I get out of these clothes," Chandler says, "and put on my pajamas?"

"Oh, God no," I say and start taking off *my* clothes to put on *my* pajamas. Chandler watches me a moment and smiles again, then goes into the bathroom with her bag to change. She's always so modest.

"I'm glad you're finally here," I say through the bathroom door.

"Yeah, our plane was late leaving New York, so I missed my connection in Brussels."

I hear her unpacking all her beauty supplies on the countertop. I back away and wait for her to come out, but she's in there awhile, and then I hear water running, and I guess she's taking a shower, so I decide to call room service and order another bowl of ice and a couple of club sandwiches.

The room-service guy is surprisingly quick, and I tip him two 5,000 lire notes. I'm just putting the lime wedges in our drinks when Chandler finally comes out of the bathroom with wet hair and wearing mint-green pajamas, the same color as the Villa Cora napkins.

"Man, I feel so much better," she says.

"I've got drinks," I say, handing her a gin and tonic. "And food."

"Thanks," she says and climbs into bed, and I climb in beside her.

We're quiet as we begin to eat. Then there's a knock on the door, and I get up to answer, and it's C. H.

"Could I come in for a minute, Sarah?" he says.

I motion with a sweep of my arm and follow him in and go back under the covers. C. H. stands with a Scotch and water at the foot of the bed looking like he's dressed for a safari, in khaki shorts and a white button-up with two big front pockets that could fit some maps and a compass.

"Chandler," C. H. says in his usual smug monotone voice, "I just wanted to say I'm sorry about your father. And, Sarah, I've heard from Paul that you haven't been out of your room since we got here. Chandler, maybe by the end of your stay you can persuade Sarah to venture outside."

"Thanks so much, Dr. Blair, for everything," Chandler says. "This is a gorgeous hotel."

"You're welcome, Chandler," C. H. says. "I have to go. Destiny's waiting for me downstairs. We're taking a walk."

I start to roll my eyes, an instinct I have when he talks about Destiny, but I stop myself and manage to smile and say, "Have a good walk, C. H."

He surprises me when he comes over and kisses my forehead before he leaves.

I take our glasses to the mini-bar to refill them. "Destiny likes to walk around nude," I say. "I mean, all day. If she's inside, the clothes are off. So now none of us kids are allowed to go see C. H. at home because if we do, we'll infringe on her nudity."

Chandler laughs. "That's crazy."

I open up a new bottle of Schweppes. "I know," I say. "And she's been going on rounds with C. H., and the night before a patient's heart surgery, if Destiny sees an aura over the patient's bed, then the operation can proceed as planned. Or it can't proceed. I can't remember if the aura is good or not. I think it is." I drop our limes in and look at Chandler as she takes a bite of her sandwich, and she starts laughing with the food in her mouth.

"Is there an aura over our bed?" she asks.

"I hope so." I smile. "Or I hope not."

We watch the orange sunset as we sip our drinks, and after the sky breaks into brilliant pinks and violets, the sun seems to disappear into the Arno. I make more drinks, and we move to the other window and watch the pool and the statues along the hedges become illuminated for the night. Then I close the shutters and the windows. "Mosquitoes," I say, and she understands.

We hang out on the bed and drink for hours watching highlights of the French Open (Agassi is already out, but Sampras has made it to the semis), until we're both drunk, and Chandler's mellow and sad, and I'm all hyper and start thinking about the animal exercise we do in class, thinking that it might help Chandler feel better and liven up.

"Robert De Niro came and spoke to us at the Actors Studio," I tell her, and I see I have her attention, "and he said that to prepare for his part in *Taxi Driver*, it helped to think of himself as a crab."

"I can see that," she says.

"Guess what animal I'd be for the role of me, Sarah Blair."

"I don't know," she says and takes a drink.

"I'll give you a hint," I say. "Room service."

Chandler reaches over for the room-service menu and studies it a moment before setting it back on the bedside table. She looks at me. "A stingray."

"How did you figure it out?"

She shrugs. "I don't know what a sea robin is, and a loin of rabbit sounds gross."

"Ah, it wasn't that bad. But it wasn't as good as the stingray." I hop to my feet and lean over, flattening my body with my arms out, letting them undulate and carry me off the bed, and I'm floating serenely around the room, low to the floor. "You see, I'm a peaceful creature, Chandler. I live on the sandy bottom in the warm shallow parts of the ocean. I won't bite. Just watch out for my tail when you go swimming, so I don't sting you, so I can keep looking for food to suck into my mouth."

"My God," Chandler says, "how do you know all that?"

I stand up and bow. "Sea World. I fed a tank of them for over an hour." I pick up my drink and sit back in bed and ask Chandler what she would be.

"I'm a cat," she says. "I'm always a cat."

"I can see that," I say. "Kind of a loner, like the stingray."

• • •

When we wake up, I tell Chandler about the hotel's complimentary limousine service and that she's welcome to go into the city if she likes, but since I'm only one day from not leaving this room for a week, I'd rather wait. I'm glad when she says that she's not ready to venture out either.

We have a late lunch of tagliarini pasta and club sandwiches, and Chandler has two Cokes because she's addicted, though she says they taste a little different here. Then we start downing mixed drinks and watch Kafelnikov and Stich play in the finals of the French Open. Kafelnikov wins in three sets, but it's close, and he becomes the first Russian ever to win the tournament. Chandler and I are happy because we were really pulling for him, clapping and whistling along with the TV crowd whenever he made a good shot.

"God, you know, with all the tennis and club sandwiches," I say, "it's like being back home in Fort Smith, Arkansas, at Hardscrabble Country Club."

"If only Leigh Ingram were here," she says, real flatly, staring at the TV. "Then we could all watch a friend wreck his car and not stop to help him and go on to lunch, and on our way back to school, see he is dead."

I'm mad at myself for bringing up Fort Smith and reminding her of her father's death, but I'm also surprised she would bring up Trey's death. We haven't spoken of it in years.

"Chandler," I say, "Trey was my boyfriend."

She turns her head, then her body, to look at me. "He was? You never told me that."

"We didn't sleep together, but we almost did. You know how you do in high school."

"I can't believe you kept it a secret, though."

"You'd gone out with him," I say.

"I wouldn't have cared."

"I didn't know that," I tell her. "And I think Leigh was with him, too, before you even."

"She was?" Chandler smiles. "He really got around."

"He was cute," I say, "and big. I felt so small when he was holding me."

Chandler rolls onto her back and is looking up at the cathedral ceiling. "I know what you mean," she says.

"Did Leigh go to your dad's funeral?" I ask, rolling onto my back and looking at the ceiling, too, wishing that I had gone. Mr. Carey's death was so sudden, and Chandler didn't call me. I had to hear what happened from C. H., and I was in New York, and all I did was send flowers.

"No," Chandler says. "But she stopped by my mom's house a few weeks ago and brought her a present from Andre's, that store with the fancy cheese and olives."

"Fort Smith has a store with fancy cheese and olives?"

"Apparently. With Leigh as the assistant manager."

"Let's call her," I say. "Let's call Leigh Ingram and see how she is. I'd like to know."

"Right now?"

"Right now," I say. "It'd be a nice thing to do."

I get the reception guy to call information in the States and connect us to Andre's. It ought to be about ten in the morning there, and Leigh should just be getting to work.

The phone rings only once before a female voice answers. "Hello," I say. "Leigh, is that you?"

"Yes," she says. "Who's this?"

"Guess," I say. "You'll never guess." But she doesn't guess, she's perfectly silent, and I say, "I'm here with Chandler," and before I can finish my sentence and tell her where I am, she says my name, incredulously, then asks if it is really me.

"Yeah, Chandler and I were just talking about you and thought we'd call to say hi."

"How long are y'all in town?"

"No, we're in Florence," I tell her. "We're trying to take it easy."

"Italy?" she says. "And you're calling *me*."

"Sure, we're calling you," I say and give the phone to Chandler, and Chandler doesn't speak at first, then thanks her for visiting her mother and starts to cry, only tears, no sound, then hands me the phone before Leigh will know.

"Leigh, it's Sarah again, how are you?"

"I'm good," she says, "I'm married. You'll have to come see me when you're in town."

"I will," I say. And I hope I will.

• • •

In the night, Chandler cries, this time loud, and I move closer to her, and I'm surprised as she takes my wrist and moves my arm around her waist, places my hand on her stomach. I have never lain like this with another woman, not even my mother when I needed her when I was young and she and C. H. divorced.

Falling asleep, I try to dream of myself as a cat, sunbathing on a diving board, with Chandler gliding below me, her dark kite shape bending in the waves from the pool boy stretching for the wall to make his turn.

• • •

It's starting to get light in the room, even with the shutters closed, when I wake at seven and notice that Chandler is not beside me. I listen and hear slight movement in the bathroom, something being picked up and put down, water trickling off an arm. I walk to the door and knock. "You all right?" I say. She doesn't answer, and I turn the knob, but it's locked.

"I'm fine," she says. "I'm taking a bath."

"Oh," I say. "I'm sorry."

"I'm thinking about going down to breakfast," she says. "I'd like to beat the crowd."

I begin to feel excited. "Can you wait for me to take a quick shower?"

"Of course," she says.

I'm pulling out clothes I think I might wear and laying them on the bed when Chandler emerges, again in her mint-green pajamas, and she's smiling and pretty, her face flushed from the hot water of her bath.

"I guess if we're getting all dressed up," she says and goes to her bag and starts pulling out her clothes, which she packed neatly by rolling them but are still wrinkled, "then I'm going to need an iron."

"In the closet," I say, as I go into the bathroom to take my shower. Shaving my legs, I think again about what I'm going to wear and decide on the cream chiffon blouse and matching ribbon-tie skirt. I put on my makeup, with brown lipstick this time, and dry my hair only halfway before getting impatient and pulling it back into a ponytail. I walk out with a towel around me, and Chandler has on a black linen dress and goes into the bathroom to do her makeup and hair.

I get dressed and slip on my snakeskin heels, then hanging up all my clothes that were on the bed, I see an orange silk sweater that I think will look good on Chandler. "You should wear this," I say and drape the sweater around her shoulders and tie it in front. Then I give her my black Gucci sunglasses, and I push them up on her head, holding back her hair. "You look beautiful, baby," I say.

She smiles, then moves to the bed and puts on ankle-strap sandals.

"Let's go," I say and grab a room key, and for the first time in a week, I'm actually going somewhere.

We walk through the lobby and out the front sliding-glass doors, past potted palms and lime trees, and step out onto the herringbone brick drive. I see a cream-colored lizard that fades into green as it scurries onto the grass and into the rosebushes. "I don't think this is the right way," I say.

"We can walk around," Chandler says.

We follow the drive that circles the hotel and pass a doorway where five or six men are sitting on a stoop, most of them smoking, dressed in white kitchen clothes and with white handkerchiefs around their necks. They eye us and say, *"Ciao, bella."*

As we walk along the pool to the restaurant, I notice that the statues I've been admiring from my room are all statues of women, some dressed, some undressed, holding bouquets of flowers, and that there are iron storks in the island of red begonias at the shallow end. And lining the boundary of the baby pool are six flags—Britain, U.S., Japan, Italy, France, and I think Germany—that I couldn't see from my window because they were blocked by an enormous tree growing out of the roof of where we are about to have breakfast.

The restaurant is like an atrium with lots of greenery and windows, and Pavarotti is playing in the background. The ceiling is painted with vines and the same verbena arbor that is on the wall above my headboard and outside by the pool.

All the tables have dark-green tablecloths with yellow place settings and silver flatware, and the chairs are wicker and tall. Even though it's not very crowded, waiters in burgundy jackets (a few I recognize) move around in a flurry, pouring coffee and hot chocolate from silver pitchers and taking away empty trays and adding new trays to the buffet.

Chandler and I sit in the corner by a window next to a handsome older couple. He's in a navy sport coat and has perfect silver hair and a slight tan, and she's wearing a short-sleeved peach suit and has shoulder-length black hair and fair skin.

Chandler leans forward. "She looks exfoliated from head to toe."

"I'm glad we dressed up," I say.

A waiter in a white jacket (the headwaiter, I guess) comes by and says, *"Buon giorno,"* then takes our napkins, unfolds them, and places them in our laps. Another waiter pours us water, and Chandler orders a Coke, and I order an espresso and an orange juice. Then we go to the buffet and fill our plates with asiago and fontina cheese, bread, rolled slices of salami and prosciutto, eggs scrambled with onions and peppers, strawberry jelly, and Nutella. When we sit down, our drinks are already here, and there's even a glass of ice for Chandler, not a bowl this time, and seeing her red aluminum Coca-Cola can among all this beauty seems funny to me and wonderful.

We eat in silence, glancing up occasionally at the other guests coming in, a woman wearing a lavender blouse and a white sweater tied, like Chandler's, around her shoulders; a young Asian couple holding hands who could be on their honeymoon.

And then I see *them*—C. H., Destiny, Whitney, Rain, Paul, and Paul's girlfriend—arrogant in their procession, dressed down in shorts and T-shirts and tennis shoes, and I stare at them for a long time as they're looking for a place to sit because it's crowded in here now, and when they finally notice me, I say, "Good morning," in this loud clear voice, and raise high my cup of espresso.

INTIMATE AND DARK

Chandler

"Can I touch your leg?" my driver asks. He's Italian, and he says it with an accent and with such confidence that I feel aroused. I also feel a little scared because there isn't a partition between us, and it's dark. I tell him to pull over. Before I get out of the car, I lean into the front seat and push my thigh toward him. He rubs it, and I stop him and get out. I don't pay. I feel I don't have to because now we are something else, closer to two people in a bar, and a free ride is a free ride.

I start walking. I turn back once and watch him drive off. For a moment, I wish he would turn around and follow me, and my escape from him would feel more heroic. I walk at a quick pace and look back again after I've gone a block. I don't see him. Home is still two blocks away.

I've taken other risks in the city, like walking in Hell's Kitchen at night or searching for a cab in the meat-packing district early enough in the morning for the transvestite prostitutes and drug dealers to still be out.

Letting that man touch my leg is a small victory. I need my pulse to quicken. I need to feel alive in the world.

Can I touch your leg? The phrase stays with me.

In my apartment, Evan, my boyfriend, is lying in bed and barely turns from the television to look at me. He removes his glasses and rubs his eyes. I walk over, climb onto him, and kiss his closed mouth.

"That's disgusting, Chandler," he says. "Take off your shoes. Do you know how dirty the streets of New York are?"

I take them off and lie next to him. I kiss his neck, and he looks above me, toward the TV. I reach down, unbutton his jeans.

He takes my wrists. "I'm not in the mood for that."

Our eyes meet, and it feels like it used to when we were first going out. Back then, when he was on top of me, he would hold down my wrists. Though this moment feels almost intimate, I break the mood and say, "My driver liked me, I think."

"Your driver?" he says. He lets go of me and gives a disapproving look.

"I couldn't get a cab. This guy from a car service pulled over and told me he'd take me." I rub my hand on his thigh.

"Relax, sweetheart. I'm doing this for us. Don't force things. It will happen. I promise." This was something Evan had said before. We had just gotten back together after a breakup. He wanted to take things slow, which meant he didn't think we should be having sex. He always made these rules and time-tables during our small breakups. One time he declared that we were not allowed to talk on the phone for three days, and another time we couldn't see each other for two weeks.

I want him to ask how my day went. Today was my last day to work at Willkie, Farr or at any law firm. I only worked there six months. I told them I just didn't like being a lawyer. They couldn't believe it. I have no idea what I'll do now.

"Do you love me?" I say.

"Yes," he says, patting my shoulder. "Now watch this, Chandler. It's interesting." He puts his glasses back on.

What we're watching is open-heart surgery on The Learning Channel.

. . .

In the morning, I wake at ten. Evan is long gone. He works in Princeton and has to take the train. He's an analyst for Merrill Lynch. It's a miserable job, at least that's what he tells me. He sometimes has to take clients out to dinner and drinks and to strip clubs. He has to go out with his boss nearly every night, while his boss picks up girls. *Has to,* he says. And he's tired, he says, and wishes he could come straight home from work and watch TV and make spaghetti. "It's a game," he tells me, when talking about his young married boss with a newborn daughter. "He's actually an all-right guy."

I reach for my Italian phrase book that I've been keeping by my bed. The summer after my father died, when I ran off to Italy and stayed with Sarah, I went out with an Italian man who drove me up into the hills, such a lush, green place, and we got out and walked into the woods and kissed. It was all I could do then. In September, I began my third year of law school, and I met Evan, and I thought my life would be good again.

Buon giorno, I say. *Grazie. Prego. Ti posso tocare en la gamba.*

Outside it's snowing, big flakes coming down like linen between the buildings. I imagine a kiss in Italy. I imagine a burst of sunlight over rows of terra-cotta roofs, salmon buildings, and green shutters.

The snow is bright and immaculate outside, but inside, my apartment seems dark and filmy. I take the rugs out to the hall and give them a shake. On hands and knees with a towel damp with hot water and Murphy Oil Soap, I scrub the floor until the scars in the wood dissolve into beveled light. In the bathroom, I scrub the bathtub and counter with Lime-Away, which has a strong pine-lime smell. I dust my dresser and bookshelf and run the dust cloth across the posters of my bed, careful because one of the knobs is loose. I pull faded green sheets from the mattress and replace them with newer peach ones and notice that it's only

11:00. I take a shower. Naked, I go back to bed. I feel good about myself. My apartment is clean and in order. I call Evan.

"Hi," I say.

"Oh, hi," he says.

"Are you busy?" I say.

"Yeah, I'll call you later."

I want to tell him I cleaned and that everything is going to be okay. I just want to tell him something.

I decide to call my friend Hugh. I call him a friend, but really he is a guy who calls me obsessively and who wants to sleep with me. I met him in a bar during a breakup with Evan and gave him my number. I had one date with him, and we got a little drunk at dinner where he told me about all the models he had dated. "Once you date one, and she trusts you, you can date any of them."

After dinner, we kissed on the street, but I wouldn't let him come up to my apartment. It was a great feeling having him want to come up, though I knew if I let him, then I would never hear from him again.

I know from my Caller ID that Hugh calls several times from work every day. I like seeing where he works, Credit Suisse, show up. He rarely leaves a message. One Saturday I spent the night out at Sarah's apartment, and saw the next morning that he called nineteen times. If I'm home when he calls, I'll pick up every once in a while, just to give him the encouragement to keep calling.

When Hugh answers the phone, I say, "Hi. I'm calling you back this time." I hear yelling in the background. Hugh works on the trading floor. He's a currency trader. There's always yelling in the background.

"Chandler," he says, "I may have to go soon, but I'll call you back. Are you at work?"

"I'm home," I say. "I quit."

"Good. You shouldn't do anything you hate. I wish I were home with you."

"You do?" I say.

"Would you like to be handcuffed where you have absolutely no control?" With the noise, he'll say anything.

"No, but I am in bed, naked, with clean sheets," I say.

"Would you like to be tied up?"

"Maybe."

"Would you like me to chain you up and put you in the corner while I watch football and eat a pizza?"

"Yes."

"We're having phone sex," Hugh says.

"Yes, we are."

"I've got to go," Hugh says.

"Oh, okay," I say.

I lie in bed and look out my window at the snow. It's really coming down. With the dark buildings, it's a perfect black-and-white postcard. I should have said something to Evan about the snow. That would have been something for him to imagine, his girlfriend watching the snow through a window.

Evan doesn't live with me, but he stays over on weekends, some work nights. Tonight he's staying at his place in Princeton. He says he needs to do things there, pay bills. He needs to check in with people. He can't always just pack a bag and take the train in. And besides, he's sick of New York.

Evan and I have been together for just over a year, though it seems much longer. After my father died, before I met Evan, I didn't want sex. Now it's something I crave. Evan says that my desire is too much, that I need to calm down.

The phone rings, and I check the Caller ID and see it's Hugh. "Do you want to have drinks," he says, "to celebrate your unemployment?"

"Definitely," I say. I tell him to meet me at Cibar at five-thirty. Hugh is almost always out of work by five.

I decide to buy a new outfit. I'm picturing myself in a skirt and these high black boots I just bought and a V-neck sweater. And a silk scarf, an Italian-looking, seductive scarf. I put on sweats and tennis shoes and go to the Agnes B. store near Union Square. I shop there fairly often, and I'm always dressed like this. I bet they wonder when I wear the clothes I buy.

I bathe for an hour. I apply makeup carefully, penciling gray liner under my green eyes. I spend twenty minutes drying my hair, watching it lighten to a dark blonde. My new sweater looks fine with the skirt and boots I have already. I'm all black, except for the burst of purple with the scarf.

Cibar is a block from my apartment and intimate and dark. I get there first. I check my coat, but leave my scarf on. I sit at the bar and order a gin and tonic. There is a group of men at a table in the corner. They are all in suits and wearing glasses and drinking beer. Hugh startles me when he kisses my cheek. "Hi, doll," he says.

"Hi," I say.

Hugh takes off his coat. He looks good in a suit.

"They fired half my group today," he says, draping his coat over a chair.

"Yeah?" I say.

He sits down. "These guys are such assholes. My manager gives this *speech*." Hugh puts on a mocking voice. "If you're still here, then you can relax. The major cuts have been made. You guys here are the new team. It's time to step up to the plate. You're in the big leagues now."

I smile. "At least you didn't get fired."

"I wish they'd fire me, then I'd get fucking four months of severance, one for every year you know, and my bonus."

"Why don't you quit, and we can go somewhere together?"

"Shit, really?" He sits back in his chair. "My bonus is coming up. Can you wait two months? Then, anywhere you want to go."

"Italy," I say.

"You got it."

Hugh leans into me, puts a hand on my leg. "In front of this bar is where we first kissed. On our one and only date."

"You're right," I say and smile, happy that Hugh remembers this, and order another drink. Hugh orders a beer, some kind of dark one on tap like the other men are drinking.

"It's really snowing," I say.

"What you need is to come home with me, stay warm, we'll hold each other all night."

"Maybe," I say.

"Oh, come on. Let me take care of you. I'll tuck you in, give you hot chocolate."

"You can come home with *me*," I say.

• • •

It's that feeling when you're in a moment, and you aren't exactly sure how you got there. I'm on top of Hugh wearing only a black camisole, my hands holding onto the headboard. And though what we're doing feels tender, and he's kissing me, and telling me I'm beautiful, I want this to be over. I want him out of my apartment. I move off of him, and he gets on top and pushes himself in again and goes slow. "Open your eyes," he says.

The phone rings. I turn my head away from him, hoping that it's Evan who's calling, but he pulls me back, starts pushing into me harder and fast, and he kisses my neck, and I feel awkward and don't want to look at him, and then he stops and shudders and pulls out of me. I turn away from him, looking at the phone.

He rubs my shoulder a moment. "Hey," he says. I don't turn around. I hear him take the condom off.

With my foot, I move my underwear until I can pull it on. I get up and check my voice mail. Evan has called saying he's already on the train, he has a meeting in the morning in the city, he'll be in around seven, but he might be late because of the snow.

I feel calm. I feel changed, somehow, and maybe when I see Evan again, we will be different.

I tell Hugh that he felt really good, that I enjoyed it, but that he's got to go. He doesn't seem to mind. He dresses quickly, then smiles as he's walking out the door. "Bye, Chandler," he says. "Bye," I say.

I pull my peach sheets off the bed, and I don't have any other clean ones, so I put on sweats and an oxford over my camisole and take the sheets to the washing machine in the basement. The smell of Hugh is on the sheets and is on me, and I'm afraid I'll run into Evan in the elevator. He stays over so often that he has his own keys, and the doorman buzzes him in automatically. It's exactly seven.

The apartment smells like smoke from the bar and cologne and sweat, and I open a window even though it's freezing outside. I take a quick shower, apply pale lipstick, dress in jeans and a black T-shirt. I spray some perfume on the clothes I was just wearing and put them in my dirty clothes basket under the green sheets from this morning. I lie across my bed but can't remain still. I get out the Lime-Away and spray the bathtub and the counter. I dust my bed and dresser and bookshelf again.

I hear the lock turn. Evan walks in wearing his black overcoat that I love. He reminds me of my father wearing his overcoat when we would take trips to New York. He never wore it much in Arkansas.

On my first date with Evan, we talked about our fathers. I told him the truth, that my father had killed himself over his failing law practice. How he'd done it in a warehouse early in the morning with a shotgun. How he'd left a letter on the kitchen table to my mother, and how I hoped to find, in my mailbox in New York, every day for weeks, a letter to me. I had been telling people that he died of a heart attack while playing golf.

Evan told me about how his father died slowly of a brain

tumor when Evan was twelve. How Evan would go to visit him in a hospital, and his father would be in a wheelchair drooling, obese from the tumor. "I was still a kid, you know," Evan said. "And this was my father. And I was embarrassed."

When I was still in law school, I would go to Princeton week-nights to see Evan. Mornings, we would make love, and I would dress in a rush, pulling on my shirt and sweater, bra in my coat pocket. We had it timed to the second, and he would drop me off just as the train braked into the station.

Coming home, tired, with his smell in my hair and my stomach still wet from when he pulled out of me, I would look out the window at the ugliness of New Jersey. I would think of the lives of the commuters, and I would want to cry for all of them. I would want to cry for sex and the closeness it was supposed to bring, but that I didn't feel. Even though he felt more inside me than anyone, it still wasn't enough.

Back then I thought Manhattan would save me. I felt like I needed the city to get lost in and forget my father and where I came from, and I felt almost happy when I would see the New Yorker hotel sign, and I'd think, *I am home, and I will never leave this place.*

"It's freezing in here," Evan says. He drops his bag and goes into the bedroom and closes the window. "Been cleaning, sweetheart?"

"Just for you," I say. I reach for him and hold on to him so tightly. I can't get close enough.

"Oh, baby," he says. "You happy to see me?"

I start crying.

"Don't cry, sugar," he says. "You have nothing to be sad about. I don't ever want to make you sad."

LATE FRAGMENT

April 1999

Chandler

On her last night in New York, Mom said she wanted to go somewhere that Sarah and I like to go, to see what my life is like here, and I didn't want to take her to Lakeside Lounge or anywhere I was sure to see someone I know, so we've come to Time Cafe and are sitting side by side at a corner booth. I'm glad she's looking around, gasping, "Oh, Chandler," at the fifties-style soda-fountain bar lined with colored seltzer bottles, at the high ceilings and carved white pillars, at the enormous white globes that hang down along with ceiling fans that shimmer whenever the subway runs underneath, at the whole southwestern undercurrent to the place, the cacti and desert tones, which she says reminds her of Oklahoma and of home.

I point above the bar at the large clock, a black-and-white one like those you see in a high-school hallway, but the hands spin fast around, then suddenly stop and move backward.

"What is that supposed to mean?" she says.

"I don't really know," I say, but I think it means that everything can be spinning along just fine, then something happens that sets you back. She must be thinking this, too, because she puts her arm around me, and I'm afraid she's going to cry. Then she lets me go and turns to look over the menu, though she is now holding my hand.

She has been holding onto me her whole visit. In Times Square for her first night, walking to see the play *Closer,* she hugged my arm in a constricting way, and I tried to keep us going at a normal pace, along with everyone else, but she barely let us move, and whenever somebody glanced at us, she said, "Good evening." And when a kind of crazy pimp-looking guy blew me a kiss and said, "You're beautiful," my mother stopped and said, "Thank you. She's my daughter."

And then there was yesterday morning when we met Sarah and her father and her father's fiancée, Destiny, at the Plaza for Easter brunch. The dining room was elegant with sprays of white lilies and ice sculptures, and they had these singing chefs who were really opera singers from the Met wearing tall white chef hats, and we were all mesmerized watching them, and I felt like it was good for my mother and me to be with people in such a setting on the third anniversary of my father's suicide, but then my mother started crying, saying it was so beautiful, then she was shaking-crying, and I had to help her from the table and guide her outside, into a cab, where she was saying, "It's not fair. Chandler, it's not fair." She kept crying and holding onto me in the cab, and I felt suffocated and helpless because I couldn't help her, almost like I didn't want to help her.

Our waiter here at Time Cafe is a young unsmiling Moroccan man who doesn't write down our order, and he quickly returns with my Coke and Mom's iced tea and two glasses of water and a bright green bottle filled with more water, and we eat bread dipped in olive oil and grated arugula, the same color as the bottle, and because Mom is looking around so much, we hardly speak.

"Chandler," she says in a hushed, almost frightened, voice, "is that the subway?"

I nod, and she presses her palms to the table to feel the vibration.

"I hope that boy can remember what we want," she says, but the waiter brings exactly what we ordered. First, two mixed green salads with balsamic vinaigrette and goat cheese. Then a pizza we're sharing that's topped with spicy chicken, poblano pepper, and black beans.

"This is delicious," Mom says. "But I can't get over this subway. Every few minutes."

As soon as she leaves tomorrow, I know I'll feel free, the way I felt as a teenager when my parents would go out for the night, and I would turn up the music and turn on all the lights and practice dancing in the long reflective den windows. And she'll be ready to leave, too, just like she was at the end of her visit last year when I saw her relief, a look that said, *I made it through this, and I won't have to come again for another year.* I don't know why she insists on flying up every Easter. It is not a holiday for us, no matter how much she tries with all her shopping to make it one. Every day we've been out to Macy's and ABC Carpet & Home where she has bought me chenille throws and decorative pillows and vases and candles and candle holders and everything else she could think of that I should not live without.

"What shall we do now?" Mom asks after paying the bill. "How about a drink at the Lakeside Lounge?"

"Well, there's kind of an interesting bar in the back," I say. "I think you'll like it."

I lead her through the arched doorway and dark narrow hall, through curtains and beads, into Fez, but when I see the couches, the mosaic wall, the brass table tops, the latticework around the windows, the gold Arabic writing above the bar, the hanging red lanterns, the portraits in gilt frames of Moroccan women with heavy eye makeup, I start to worry that maybe this is not the place for my mother. That Fez is too foreign, and the people too young, that it will make her feel too old, and I start to feel old and out of place here myself, but then she raises her

146

eyebrows and says, "Wow, Chandler, it's like we're in *Casablanca* or *Lawrence of Arabia* or something."

From out of nowhere a woman close to my mother's age chimes in with a loud, drawn-out, twangy "I know." And then her husband, with light brown hair swept gracefully to the side and behind his ears, introduces himself and his wife and holds his hand out to my mother. "You sound like you're from our neck of the woods," he says, then says they're from Texas, and Mom tells him we're from Arkansas, and the husband and wife grin, like it's a small world. Then the man introduces their son and their son's wife, who are living in New York, and they nod to us. They are a perfect-looking family. A beautiful couple my age and a beautiful couple Mom's age.

I step up to the bar and order two gin and tonics. And while I'm paying the bartender, I hear my mother telling them about my graduating from NYU law school but how I quit being a lawyer—just didn't like it—and am now proofreading at an investment bank right across from the World Trade Center. Surely, she won't tell them, too, how I don't have a boyfriend, not since Evan, but she doesn't. She begins telling a story about our first time to visit New York with my father. I hate to even turn around and be a part of this. When I was young at tennis tournaments, my mom would tell a waitress or anyone who would listen about who I beat in my first-round match, who I might play in the semifinals, what I was seeded. But I do turn around, I have to turn around, and join the circle. Mom takes her drink but doesn't stop talking to drink it.

"Chandler," she says, "do you remember that pretty stewardess pointing out all the buildings in the skyline?"

I nod and sip my drink, though I don't remember.

"It was at night," she says.

Then I do remember. The stewardess pointed out the white pyramid of light that was the Chrysler Building, which I see now and still find myself gazing at whenever I'm walking home on Irving from Union Square, and then she pointed out the red, white, and blue of the Empire State Building, though during Christmas it's lit red and green, and the stewardess said she lived right there in the middle. I couldn't imagine anyone living there.

"On that trip," my mother says, "we stayed at the Waldorf."

"Oh, I love the Waldorf," the older woman says.

"It's one of her favorite hotels," her husband says.

"But the next year when we came, about the same time, in February I think," says Mom, "we stayed at the Grand Hyatt, which had nice rooms but was by Grand Central Station, an area that made me feel a little uneasy right off the bat."

The son and daughter-in-law begin to look elsewhere, and I feel bad for them and hope Mom will just stop talking and let these poor people move on.

"Anyway," she says, "it had just started snowing, and Chandler and I were walking back to the Grand Hyatt after shopping, and I was carrying these Saks bags, and we were holding a big black umbrella between us, and Chandler had one of those little girl purses," and she reaches out and touches the daughter-in-law on the arm to get her attention. "You remember those little girl purses, right? Small on a long thin strap? And it was swinging back and forth because she was really walking. Chandler's always walked fast."

The daughter-in-law smiles and nods, probably afraid not to. And so does her husband.

"And then from out of nowhere," says Mom, "I saw this *black* arm come up from behind us trying to get that purse. I mean, it was *black*, like a *black* snake."

I cannot believe she would emphasize or even mention the word *black*, and I feel sick and out of breath, yet none of them seem fazed or bothered and keep listening.

"But I was also afraid he was trying to get Chandler," my mother says, "so I pulled her to me so hard that we slipped and fell, really causing a commotion, then I became a tiger, swinging my arms trying to claw and grab at him, just like a mama tiger, screaming for him to get away. And he did. He held up his hands, like *Whoa, mama,* then backed away and ran. Then I'm telling you the best-looking man I've ever seen with the best-looking clothes and haircut helped us up.

"And when we got back to our hotel room and told Chandler's father what had happened, the first thing he said was, 'You mean that man who helped you was better looking than I am?'"

They laugh, and I laugh.

"And you know what that guy, the pickpocket, would have found in Chandler's purse?" Mom asks.

"No," the couples say.

"Chewing gum and a pack of cards."

Everybody laughs, and I smile at the young couple, and they smile back at me, then Mom says it was nice meeting them all, and she takes a sip of her drink as we move to a table.

"Mom," I whisper, leaning into her, "you did a great job telling that story. But at first, I had no idea where you were going."

She smiles. "I know you didn't."

• • •

Mom lingers on the stoop of my building and gazes at the spindly budding trees and cast-iron fence of Gramercy Park, which is dimly lit by the faint glow of street lamps.

"It's really lovely here, Chandler," she says. "Just think, Oscar Wilde lived here and Edith Wharton, and now you. Come on," she says, motioning for me to join her, "let's take a walk around the park."

I point out my favorite buildings in the neighborhood as we

pass them: the Brotherhood Synagogue, the red-brick apartment building that stretches back a block with the octagonal turrets, the broad white terra-cotta apartment building with the suits of armor standing guard out front, the Gramercy Park Hotel, the National Arts Club, and then, of course, home, and Mom sighs, and Mohammed, the doorman, buzzes us in.

As soon as we get up to my apartment, Mom puts on her nightgown and I put on pajamas, and we light my new scented candles, two orange and clove in silver candlesticks, and one lavender held in a square mosaic of iridescent glass. My mother keeps rearranging the candles, and soft light flickers against her face and blonde highlights.

"This is what I like to do at home," she says. "Candles give me so much pleasure. And when I'm gone, you can light these candles, and maybe they will make you happy, too."

Then she looks at my bookcase and discovers the book she gave me about Raymond Carver. The book is called *Carver Country: The World of Raymond Carver,* and on the cover is a picture of him smoking with his hand covering all of his face but his eyes, which are confident and unashamed, as if he knows he should care but doesn't care, four years before his death, that smoking will kill him. She holds the book to her chest as she gets under the covers.

"Chandler, do you remember when I gave this to you?"

"Not really," I say, walking over to her.

"Here," and she hands me the book, open to the inscription *To Chandler, Love, Mom, Christmas 1995.*

I look at her, and her gold-green eyes tear up and turn greener, green like mine.

"Will you sleep in here with me tonight?" she says.

"Okay," I say. "But I'm a light sleeper, you know."

"I know," she says, patting the place next to her.

I lay the book on the bedside table, then go around and blow out all the candles before I climb in. We lie still, but after a moment she asks me if we can lie on our sides and if I will put my arm around her.

"Sure," I say, and I do, and I try not to cry because she is crying. I hold her that way for a long time, as long as I can, until she stops crying and begins to twitch, then lightly snores, and I move away and go into the other room with the Raymond Carver book, what Mom gave me, which I had forgotten, that last Christmas, when everything was fine, was great, with Mom bringing in popcorn and Cokes and homemade fudge to my dad and me while we played cards all day every day I was home.

I get into the sofa bed and look through the pages at pictures of Carver's friends and family, letters, fragments from stories and poems, at his whole life. Then at the end there is a picture of his wife sitting at his grave, crying, her hand over her mouth. Beside it there is this poem, "Late Fragment":

> And did you get what
> you wanted from this life, even so?
> I did.
> And what did you want?
> To call myself beloved, to feel myself
> beloved on the earth.

I think about my mother and father, about that Christmas before everything fell apart, about Sarah, about tennis and high school and Leigh and Trey, about Sewanee and Washington and New York and Florence, about failed love and gin rummy, about how everything stopped and has been moving backward, about the last line of that poem, which I wonder if I am beginning, once again, to travel toward.

THE KIND OF GIRL HE PLAYS GUITAR FOR

NOVEMBER 1999

Leigh

I keep my eyes closed and lie perfectly still, trying not to give myself away, but Cassidy keeps moving his hand under my nightgown. It's been like this for a while now, him always wanting sex. It used to be different. I used to be the one to wake him up, run my hand over his thigh, moving closer, until he would grab me and move me on top of him. I don't really understand what's wrong. I love Cassidy. It's just that I don't feel aroused. I never want to touch him or kiss him for long, though sometimes I give in, and we make love once a week or so.

I roll over, away from Cassidy, but he's persistent, so I flinch like I'm feeling him for the first time and open my eyes, and he's sitting over me, smiling, or trying to smile. His goatee is only a week old, so I'm not used to it yet, and it still makes him look mean. I reach under my gown and take hold of his hand.

"Oh, Cassidy, not today, okay? It's Thanksgiving." I feel I have a good excuse, since I've been a little stressed out about spending the day with Mom and her new boyfriend I haven't met yet, this refrigerator salesman at Sears she's been seeing seriously a few months now. She's back at Penney's, though this time selling shoes.

He stops smiling, and his hand and arm slink lifelessly away. "You know, girls at Old Town don't find me so untouchable."

I hate that he says this because he's said this to me before, as if I am not twenty-nine years old but twenty-one, the kind of girl I used to be, who was in awe, I guess, just because he was in a band, which is the kind of girl he plays guitar for night after night—though not every night. His day job is still at Movieland. He only plays at Old Town two or three nights a week, but not even for a cut of the cover. It's just pass the hat, and after the band splits it four ways, what Cassidy usually comes home with is about eight dollars, and he's drunk, since they get their drinks on the house. Twenty dollars if he's lucky.

"You'd be proud of me," he says, sinking back, with his elbows in his pillow and his head against the headboard, "last night this knockout chick was putting her hand on my leg and asking me to go back to her place." He laughs. "Her parents' place, really. But see how devoted I am? I love you. You love me, right?"

"Yeah," I say. I throw the tangled covers off my legs and glance at the clock. "We need to start getting ready."

● ● ●

Mom's duplex neighbor has got quite a crowd over. Cars are lined up in the driveway and parked in the yard and on both sides of the street. But at Mom's, so far it's just Mom, and the sight of her new silver Nissan Altima still strikes me as strange, and I feel full of hope for her and a little jealous, too, as Cassidy pulls up the drive behind it. I didn't think Mom would ever give up on Chryslers, but her boyfriend, Roy, has a Nissan Altima himself and is good friends with the floor manager at Nissan, so he was able to get her a good price on one.

"Maybe Roy can help us get a good deal on one of those," I say.

Cassidy shrugs. "I don't know," he says and pats the cracked, sun-warped dash of my Honda. "It's nice not having a payment."

"Yeah," I say, unbuckling myself and taking my Andre's sack in my arms, "but it's nice to have nice things, too, you know." I get out and slam my door, because you have to slam the door, and he slams his.

Mom's in the kitchen standing by the oven with a glass of wine in her hand, with her other hand resting on her hip, and she's dressed in her usual attire, a tight black top tucked into jeans, with high-heeled black ankle boots, and I know, even with the Nissan, even with the boyfriend, she is never going to change.

"It's just going to be us," she says, then slugs back her wine.

I'm suddenly dreading the day here without Roy. "What happened?" I ask.

"Hi, Suzanne," says Cassidy, breezing around me, heading toward the den to watch television. He likes the parades.

"I like your goatee, Cassidy," Mom says. Then in a sing-songy voice, she says, "Cass-i-dy," and he turns around. She points her empty glass toward the refrigerator. "Help yourself to the wine, handsome. There's plenty."

"And I want plenty," he says, backing up and reaching for the cabinet with the wine glasses.

"I brought wine, too," I say. I set the pretty forest-green sack on the counter and take everything out and show her the bottle of St. George Merlot with the nice gold label that I bought at Andre's with my employee discount. "It's one of our best-selling wines," I say.

She wrinkles up her face and puts her hand around the bottle. "It's not even cold yet. Put it in the refrigerator, and maybe we can try it with dinner."

"But it's not supposed to be chilled," I tell her.

"I like mine chilled," says Cassidy.

"Oh, me, too," says Mom, watching Cassidy search in the refrigerator, behind the milk and ketchup and jar of pickles.

"I don't see it," he says.

"It's down below, in the box," she says.

"Oh," he says and bends down and taps Ernest & Julio Gallo Rosé into his glass.

"Fill me up again, will you, dear?" Mom says, and Cassidy sets his glass on the floor between his cowboy boots, then takes her glass, and while he's filling her up again, she shifts her eyes at me. "Don't you want some, too?"

"Maybe later," I say.

"Later?" Mom shakes her head. "I hate the holidays."

"Yeah, what's Thanksgiving?" says Cassidy, standing up with both glasses and swinging the refrigerator door closed with the heel of his boot.

Mom takes her glass from him and asks if he'll change the lightbulb on the front porch and light the fireplace pilot for the gas logs before dinner, which is about thirty minutes away. She almost always has something for him to do, some little job she thinks is better done by a man. As soon as Cassidy is out the door with the stepladder and a lightbulb, I ask her again, "What happened?"

Mom picks up a potholder, one of the ones I made in fourth grade out of red and blue yarn, a crooked square with an uneven pattern. They were for an economics project, and every day after school I would rush home and go straight to my room to weave.

Mom lifts the lid off the pot of bubbling creamed corn. "I don't know," she says, stirring. "He called just a few minutes ago, said he wasn't feeling well or something. He sounded fine to me. I thought it was working out for us."

"Well, it still might be," I say. "Roy might really be sick, you know."

"I don't know. I don't think so," she says. "We had some words." She covers the corn, then lifts the lid off the gravy and begins stirring it.

"What did you say?" I ask.

"Oh, let's not talk about it. I don't feel like talking about it."

"All right," I say, and looking at her this close, I'm surprised to see so much gray starting to show in her brown hair, still thick and straight and styled like she could be in her twenties.

I reach over the corn and peel back the aluminum foil to look at her dressing. She doesn't make it the way Cassidy's mother makes it, with homemade cornbread. Mom does it with Pepperidge Farm Croutons, which I like a lot better.

"What can I do to help?" I ask, and I take a spoon of dressing from the corner of the pan, and it melts in my mouth with the flavor of chicken broth.

"You can set the table," she tells me.

I fold the foil back over the pan. "Okay," I say, giving her a smile.

She nods, kind of distantly, and I go to the drawer with my old potholders and take out three napkins, three napkin rings, and three place mats.

While I set the table, I listen to the pregame football talk filter through the walls from next door. Something about special teams and running it all the way back. Cassidy comes in from outside to throw away the bad lightbulb and put the stepladder in the pantry. He stops to pick up his glass of wine and sips on it as he heads into the den.

Mom bastes the turkey, then slides it back into the oven. "Just a few more minutes," she says, then opens the refrigerator and refills her glass.

I wander into the den but not because Cassidy is there striking a match against the hearth and not because I want to watch the Macy's Thanksgiving Day Parade. I'm not sure why I'm in the den. I don't know where I want to be. I don't want to sit, so I stop in front of Mom's china cabinet and look at the breakables on display that she has collected her whole life.

On the top shelf there's the beginning of a state plate collection, five in all, souvenirs from trips with boyfriends. The one with the cleaver-shaped state of Oklahoma is the first one she bought, just across the border in Pocola, and when she went to Six Flags, she brought back one with a mockingbird, the state bird of Texas. Then when she went to Memphis to see the Rossington Collins Band, she got the third one, with the state bird of Tennessee, also a mockingbird. The other two plates are from here in Arkansas, from a truck stop on the way to the horse races in Hot Springs, and though they both bear the state bird, more mockingbirds, there is a difference between them: one says *The Land of Opportunity,* the original state motto, and the other says *The Natural State,* the revised state motto.

Mom finds this state-bird business funny and wants to take a trip to Mississippi some day just so she can have another mockingbird plate for the top shelf, but it all makes me kind of sad. She keeps saying she's going to throw away the Oklahoma plate because it looks out of place, and I keep telling her to throw them all out. But here they are, still just inches above my yellow toothpick house that I built in the sixth grade, the centerpiece on the second shelf, which I am glad she's kept, like my potholders.

I remember my teacher Mrs. Hill telling us to buy a box of toothpicks and a bottle of glue but wouldn't tell us why, not at first. Then one day in art she went around and gave each student a board, about eight inches long and six inches wide, and said that we were going to learn a lesson that day, and for every day that week, and for every day the following week, on patience.

We could build anything we wanted to build on that board. If I'd thought of a stack of money like one of my friends did, I might have done that, but what came to my mind first was a house. I'd lived in an apartment and then this duplex, but nothing like the yellow two-story house I built with real shutters that open and close and are painted black, nothing that comes close to this house I built with a garage and a garage door, with a fenced backyard, with nice thick green even grass, with my very own yellow dog and yellow doghouse.

I open the china cabinet to get a better look at what I still don't have, but Mom calls out that dinner is ready, so I close it back, and as I follow Cassidy past the fireplace into the kitchen, I feel the heat from the gas logs.

"I need a strong man to carry the turkey to the table," says Mom, smiling at Cassidy, though I see she's already carried it from the cooking pan to the platter. I go to my bottle of Merlot on the counter and fold out the corkscrew I brought that says Andre's along the side in gold lettering.

"Why don't you carve it for us, too," Mom tells him.

I'm hunched all over the bottle, gripping it in a headlock and turning the screw slowly into the cork as I watch Cassidy take the knife and fork into his hands and try to visualize where to start.

Mom pulls out a chair and sits down and lights a cigarette, while Cassidy continues to aim and re-aim, and before he ever pierces the skin of the turkey, I pop the cork, and they both turn around.

"Wine anybody?" I ask.

"I'm good," says Cassidy.

Mom takes a long drag on her cigarette and arches her eyebrows at me. "All right," she says, then releases smoke from the corner of her mouth, "I'll give it a shot." She downs the last of her rosé and holds up her glass, and I walk over and fill it halfway, a dark-cherry color.

"I think you'll like it," I say. "It's really good."

Mom raises the glass to her nose. "It's not going to be sweet, is it?"

"Not as sweet as yours," I tell her.

"And not as good as yours either," says Cassidy.

"Nevermind him," I say. "You get used to it after a few sips. It gets better and better, actually." I sit at my place at the table and fill my glass, and I watch Mom take the smallest taste of the wine, and she sets the glass down and goes back to her cigarette.

I cross my legs and enjoy my wine—so what if it's fancy?—and Cassidy is finally carving into the breast meat, and I watch steam rise like all the smoke in here. Mom holds up her plate, and Cassidy serves her some turkey, and then he does the same for me, and once he has served himself a leg, he sits down, too, at the head of the table, and we begin helping ourselves with the rest of the food.

"Well," says Mom, slipping her napkin out of her napkin ring and spreading it across her lap, as the rest of us are doing, "maybe next year we'll have Thanksgiving at y'all's place."

"I offered this year, remember?" I say.

"It would be nice not to have to do all the work again," she says and slides her fork into her mashed potatoes. "It's tiring, you know. You'll see."

"Whatever," I say.

"I earned my keep today at least, though, didn't I, Suzanne?" Cassidy says.

Mom leans over and slaps his leg. "Absolutely, hon. You're quite the handy man."

I reach for my wine, realizing I should've started drinking earlier, and when I finish my glass, Mom asks if I want hers.

"You don't like it?" I say.

"No, it's not for me," she says.

She empties her glass into mine, then gets up to refill hers and Cassidy's from the wine box in the refrigerator. Then we're quiet for a while, eating, and then Mom sets her silverware down, leaving her food half-eaten like she always does, and lights another cigarette.

"What I need is *me* a Cassidy," she says.

"What?" I say. I look at Cassidy, and he smiles.

"I like to go to Old Town. Really, Cassidy," she says, touching his arm, "I'm a little in love with you."

"Mom, God!" I say. I've seen her drunk this way with a lot of men, but never with Cassidy.

"Oh, you know what I mean."

"No, I don't," I tell her. "That's creepy."

Cassidy's laughing, and I tell him to stop.

"Oh, give her a break," he tells me. "She doesn't mean it that way."

"That's right," Mom says. "I just need somebody who's still young and fun and not always talking about how many damn refrigerators he needs to sell or what his goddamn children might think of us. You don't know how lucky you are, Leigh. I can tell you just don't." She leans over to Cassidy and hangs an arm around his shoulders. "Your band rocks," she tells him.

"We try," he says.

"I mean, you really rock," she says, and he nods, smiling, and she is smiling. "You're cooler than every guy out there, Cassidy. I mean, I love what you stand for."

"Thanks, Suzanne," he says.

"What do you stand for, Mom?" I say.

She sits back in her chair and shifts her eyes in my direction as she draws on her cigarette. "You're being too sensitive, Leigh."

"Yeah," says Cassidy. "She's just fooling around. Trying to make Thanksgiving fun."

Then he leans over and kisses me on the mouth, slipping his tongue in a moment, and I'm embarrassed, but my mother is smiling, like this is romantic, like she is happy for us.

"So tell me," he says, sitting back down and spooning a second helping of corn onto his plate, "what kind of music does this Roy listen to?"

"Oh," says Mom, "he likes country, like I do sometimes, and like you do, Cassidy, but he really likes big band."

"Wow," Cassidy says. "How old is he?"

"He's fifty like me. But he *acts* fifty."

"I bet his kids appreciate that," I say.

"I don't ever want to listen to big band," Cassidy says. "So, Suzanne, is this Roy at least good to you?"

"Oh, he is. And he's a wonderful lover."

I clang my knife and fork onto my plate. "You didn't want to talk to me about Roy when I asked you about him, but you'll say what a great lover Roy is to Cassidy?"

Mom takes a drink of her wine, then says, "No, I said *wonderful* lover."

Cassidy laughs, and I shoot him a look.

"What?" he says casually. "She did say wonderful."

"You tell her, Cassidy," Mom says.

And that's it for me. I get up from the table. I go to the counter and cork the wine and put the bottle in my Andre's sack, along with the corkscrew, and grab the bag of freshly ground Banana-Nut Coffee that I brought and set out and no one said a word about.

Cassidy and Mom watch me and start laughing.

Then I open the kitchen drawer with my potholders, and I put my potholders in my Andre's sack. Then I see one on the counter, and I take it, too, then I see one under the pot of green beans on the table, and I take that one.

"Oh, you're so dramatic," laughs Mom. And Cassidy is pounding her rickety cheap kitchen table with his fist and sloshing their wine and even the gravy.

I turn around and collect my sack and head into the den.

"What are you doing?" Mom yells, but I don't answer.

I go to the china cabinet and swing open the door and grab my toothpick house by the base and steady it in my free hand.

Patience, I tell myself, walking back into the kitchen. Patience. Patience.

When they see me, Cassidy and Mom start howling and pointing at me and my Andre's sack and my toothpick house. And Mom starts shoving his shoulder, it's just so funny, and he shoves her.

With the hand holding the sack, I scoop up my purse. "You two just laugh it up together in this half of a house and talk about Roy with your plate collection."

I go outside and set the toothpick house on the roof of my car and get out my keys. I imagine the crowd next door is getting along the way some families have to be getting along, seeing as all the cars are still parked all over the place, and then I see there's even another one parked on the street, on our side, the bumper almost blocking me in. It will not be easy trying to get out of here.

THE SPACE BETWEEN US

Sarah

I'm standing out in front of the Fort Smith airport feeling weird, looking around at this hot flat desolate place, the half-empty parking lot, and beyond that the service road and the highway, the low hills and treetops, which I haven't seen in five years, or been allowed to really, and I'm a little disappointed in myself that I'm even here this time to attend C. H.'s sixth wedding, which will take place in the backyard of the house I grew up in, the house I've been banned from for five years because Destiny is a nudist. Apparently, for the wedding weekend, so that Paul and Whitney and I can return home, Destiny has agreed to wear a bathrobe.

My flights from New York to Memphis and Memphis to here were as empty as this parking lot, so I got to sleep some, having the whole row on both flights to myself, so I'm feeling okay, well-rested, I mean, ready to face my family, I suppose, if somebody will just pick me up soon out of this heat. I hope somebody remembers to pick me up.

A silver Porsche whips into the loading zone right in front of me, but it's not a car I recognize. Then I see it's my brother Paul, wearing a baseball cap and finishing off a Heineken.

"Sarah, hey," he says, his voice booming as he gets out.

I walk over to him. "Paul," I say, and we hug.

163

He bends down for my bag, then puts it in the trunk. "Hope you haven't been waiting out here too long."

"Not really," I say. "Gave me a chance to admire the scenery."

"Well, good." He opens my door for me like we're on a date.

"Thank you," I say. "Nice car."

"It's one of C. H.'s," he says, then closes my door and runs around to the other side and gets in. "Only a year old. He just gave it to me yesterday when he picked me up at the airport."

I guess I'm not really surprised by this. C. H. never gives anybody a birthday gift, but sometimes out of the blue he'll give you a new Rolex or Louis Vuitton luggage, or a car. "Great," I say and buckle my seat belt. "Guess I should've gotten here yesterday."

"Guess so," he says and shifts into first and starts driving. "Guess who gets to be best man?"

"You," I say.

"Nope," he says. "Dwane does."

"Who's Dwane?"

"Destiny's homeless brother, though I guess he's homeful now. He's been staying with C. H. for the last month."

"Is he really homeless?" I say.

"Well, not on the street or anything. I think he just goes around from place to place and tries to stay for free with people. He's actually kind of nice. And he's been working in the yard."

"Great," I say.

"He used to be addicted to crack or something, but he's kicked the habit."

"Wonderful," I say.

Paul pulls into a drive-thru liquor store and gets a six-pack of cold Heineken for now, then some Absolut and Bombay Sapphire for later.

We drink our beers, and Paul turns up the music, the Sex Pistols, which he tells me he's playing for my benefit, and I sing and scowl and shake my head along with him for a while, then I stop because I get distracted looking around at Fort Smith, how it's changed and not changed, with new restaurants and hotels in the same old buildings but now with different names.

When we're on East Valley Road, about to make our turn, everything looks exactly the same, our house almost hidden from the road with the rising driveway that winds around through white oaks and the one river birch that Mom and I planted when I was a kid, and when we get closer the house looks longer than I remembered, though I know it isn't, and I see that the dull gray bricks have been painted a nice soft yellow, and planted in front of the hedges now are brilliant bursts of red salvias and yellow marigolds, and baskets on the porch overflow with pink and violet impatiens and petunias. Even the lawn looks immaculate, the old tire ruts erased where C. H.—instead of following the drive as it curves to the far right side of the house to the three-car garage—always pulls onto the yard to park as close to the front door as possible. I don't think the grass has ever looked this green and fresh and full.

"The house looks beautiful," I say.

"All thanks to Dwane," Paul says.

Paul pulls up in the garage, and it looks like we're the only ones here. He carries my bag for me, and we walk through the garage door into the kitchen, which has been redecorated in a kind of Chinese-restaurant way with reds and golds.

"So, what do you think?" Paul asks.

"I think it looks stupid," I say. "It totally doesn't match the outside."

"Wait and see the rest of it," he says, waving for me to follow.

At first, I think the living room looks okay, with Oriental rugs and antique couches, but then I see there's a lacquered black and, I guess, very expensive four-poster day bed with a canopy, and the wood everywhere is hand-painted, decorated with horses and with men in armor having sex with scantily clad concubines. I give him a look.

"I thought you'd like that," he says.

I walk behind him down the long hall, which is the way to all the bedrooms, and he leads me to my old room, and my old bed is here, in the corner against the wall, but now there's a small mahogany desk beside it and a matching bookcase filled with nice hardbacks you can tell come in a set, classics by authors like Melville, Twain, and Dickens.

"Welcome to Destiny's writing room," Paul says.

"I didn't even know she read."

"She doesn't," he says, "but she saw a writing room in some decorating magazine and decided that she had to have one."

"Great," I say.

Paul sets my bag down and turns to go out, then we hear a door open on the other side of the house and a faint hello. Destiny.

Paul yells hello back, and we walk down the hall and meet Destiny, Whitney, Rain, and Dwane in the living room, Dwane already stretched out on the day bed.

Whitney, whom I haven't seen for two years since she came to New York and stayed with me for the U.S. Open and who wouldn't even buy me a baked potato there for lunch and made me lose my place in the food-court line and have to go all the way over by the front gate to an ATM machine to get some cash, walks over and gives me a fake hug, and I give her a fake hug back. She has a new haircut, shoulder-length, and also has a few blonde highlights, but her hair still looks brown, not blonde all over like mine. "Cute hair," I say. Then Destiny hugs me, and I think she has a new haircut, too, angled at the chin and dyed even darker, and then I notice Rain has shorter hair, with red highlights, and I realize that they've all just spent the afternoon at the hair salon and didn't even bother to ask if I wanted to come. Not that I would have taken an earlier flight. Still.

I turn to Dwane. "I hear you're the best man."

"Sure am," he says, "and Paul's going to stand up there with me."

"Sure am," Paul says, and he high-fives Dwane, like he and Dwane have suddenly become friends, then Rain chimes in that she is the maid of honor and that Whitney is going to stand next to her, but that it's all real casual, just in the backyard and all.

"You can stand up there with the girls if you like," Destiny tells me.

"Oh, no," I say. "Thanks for asking, though." I'm starting to feel like I may cry, and I am really wanting to get the hell out of the room. "I'm going to unpack," I say. "If you need me, I'll be in the writing room."

Then I go to my room, and I stay in my room, and I lie on my bed and close my eyes and imagine my room as it used to be, the way Mom decorated it—with a little yellow dresser trimmed in white and a wicker bookcase that I used as a trophy case that was packed full of tennis trophies—gold and silver statues on marble bases, silver platters, and one silver goblet that I won at the Easter Bowl. When Mom left us in high school to move to D.C., Barry was already away at college, and she didn't even ask me to go with her. She and C. H. thought it would be best that I stay and finish high school in Fort Smith. It's what I would have wanted to do even if I'd been asked, but it would have been nice to have been asked. And when I left for college, I told C. H.'s wife at the time that she could just give away my furniture and throw out all my trophies.

I look around at Destiny's bookcase, and she actually has a few readable books in here, and I read *Franny and Zooey*, the whole book, a book I love and have read many times before, and I don't see another family member for the rest of the night, not even C. H., even though I hear his voice in the hall when he comes in late from the hospital, not even when I sneak into the kitchen and make a peanut butter and jelly sandwich and a vodka tonic. I sure wish I could be drinking my vodka tonic out of that goblet.

. . .

It's always bright in my room in the morning, and because it faces the golf course, it can be a little loud on Saturdays, so I'm already awake when C. H. knocks on my door and asks to come in.

"Sweet Sarah," he says and bends down to give me a kiss on my forehead.

"Hi, C. H.," I say, and I see he's dressed in an all-white Fila outfit, the shorts, the polo shirt, even his shoes. He sits on the bed beside me.

"How was your flight?" he asks.

"Fine," I say. "Easy."

"Good." He smiles. "How about a family tennis match in say thirty minutes?"

"I didn't bring a racquet," I tell him, though I'm prepared to play. I've been taking lessons lately in New York from this Australian guy who just stopped playing the pro tour.

"Well, I just bought two new ones," he says, "Völkls, from Germany. That's what you play with, right?"

"Yeah," I say, and I'm surprised and even touched he remembered.

C. H. grips my arm, then pats it. "All right, kiddo," he says, standing up and walking toward the door. "Get moving."

He shuts the door behind him, and I get right up and put on shorts and a T-shirt, and I'm feeling so excited about playing that I almost race down the hall to the bathroom to get all ready, putting my hair in a ponytail with two barrettes on each side, so there's no chance that even a strand of hair will fall in front of my eyes when I serve.

Once I have my tennis shoes on, I go into the kitchen to grab a quick, healthy breakfast of orange juice and a slice of wheat toast. I'm wondering where everyone is, then I realize that they must be in the backyard, getting things prepared for the evening ceremony. I walk outside and they're all there, ordering workmen where to put these pretty wooden chairs with white cushions, where to set up these tall silver candelabras to mark where Dwane and Paul, then where Whitney and Rain, will stand, and C. H. and Destiny will be right there in the middle, and I'll be on the front row somewhere, I guess, with any of C. H.'s family or friends who aren't too tired yet of coming to these things.

"Hey, Sarah," Paul says, walking over, "it's me and you against C. H. and Whitney."

"Oh, good," I say, and I give him a high-five.

• • •

We drive the two-minute drive to Hardscrabble the way we're divided into teams, with C. H. and Whitney up front and Paul and me in back, and we don't talk, like we're all gearing up for a big match, and I keep wondering if this black BMW will ever become mine or Whitney's.

The courts are all empty, so we get to play on the best one, the one with lots of shade that's close to the good water fountain. And while C. H. stretches, Whitney tells Paul and me that after the ceremony everybody will get driven over in golf carts from our house up to Hardscrabble's clubhouse for the reception, which I have to admit sounds kind of fun. I haven't ridden in a golf cart since I was a kid and was always trying to par the lake hole.

C. H. has to stretch for about twenty minutes before playing. The funniest stretch he does is when he rests one leg on the net and rotates his arms quickly in a one-two motion like he's swimming free-style. He even says, "One two, one two," while he's doing it. Paul and I always laugh during this, and C. H. always completely ignores us. Once we get on the court, I warm up against Whitney, and I can't believe how good she is. I think I could still beat her in singles, but she is really hitting the ball deep with a lot of topspin, and I'm starting to feel tired because neither of us has missed yet. I glance over at Paul, and I see he misses the ball completely, and then he slips, getting a streak of green clay on his shorts, and Whitney and I both start laughing, and I completely mishit the ball to the other court.

C. H. doesn't even notice because he's in a zone over there warming up his shoulder with his service motion. Then he stops and looks at us. "I'm ready to start whenever you are," he says.

"What the hell," Paul says. "Let's go."

I spin my racquet. "Up or down," I say.

"Up," Whitney says.

I look at the design on the base of the grip. "Nope, it's down," I say. "We'll serve."

I let Paul serve first, and he's so rusty that he double-faults the whole game away, and then C. H. double-faults most of his game away, so we're tied up, and Whitney and I both win our serves, and the games go like that for a while until it's 4-all. Then Paul's serve just suddenly clicks, and he hits two aces and wins the other two points in baseline rallies. Paul is so happy that he does a little jump and rushes over to me and we high-five, and C. H. and Whitney are just standing there, and Whitney says, "The set's not over, you know."

"We know," Paul says and hits two balls over to C. H.

"Third ball, please," C. H. says. He likes to make sure all the balls have even play. Whitney has the third ball in her pocket and throws it to him. Then Paul and I start laughing because we always laugh about this third-ball stuff, and C. H. gets mad, and when he serves he serves the ball so far out that it hits the back fence without bouncing first. His second serve is soft, and Paul just kills it right down the line past Whitney, who doesn't say good shot or anything. And when C. H. serves to me, I hit my return past Whitney, too, and then C. H. double-faults twice to lose the set.

I try to be nice and say, "Good set. Want to play another one?" But C. H. and Whitney say they want to get home, that there's a lot to do at home.

"Okay," I say, and I shake Paul's hand, and we make a move toward the net, and I'm relieved that Whitney and C. H. go up to the net as well and shake our hands.

Paul and I decide to walk home later after we have lunch at the snack bar, but we promise C. H. that we'll be ready for the ceremony at six o'clock. I haven't been up to the snack bar in ages. But it looks exactly the same, lots of young mothers, all in bathing suits with matching cover-ups, with their kids running around wild and their husbands sitting back at the wrought-iron tables with the green-and-white umbrellas.

For lunch, Paul and I both have chicken fingers and fries and strawberry daiquiris.

"You know," I say, waving my plastic glass around, "I haven't had a single strawberry daiquiri the whole time I've lived in New York."

Paul takes the orange slice from the rim of his daiquiri and bites into it before taking a drink. "I haven't either. In Dallas, I mean," he says. "What about auditions? Ever met anybody famous at one?"

"One time," I say, "I saw Susan Sarandon. I got on the elevator with her, rode two floors, and couldn't think of a thing to say. I was up for the part of her daughter."

He dips a fry in his cup of ketchup. "I could see that."

"I think I got close. The casting director told me she would recommend me for another part, but I don't think she did."

Paul smiles at me, and I want to tell him something else about my life in New York, how it's lonely there in my apartment sometimes. How all the rejection is hard to take.

"Let's hit some range balls," Paul says. "I haven't done that in a while."

"Yeah," I say, "I haven't done that in forever."

We borrow a couple of 7 irons from the golf pro shop and hit range balls for the rest of the afternoon, six baskets full, each swinging in our own meditative rhythm, hitting Titleists toward our childhood home that shows yellow through the trees.

• • •

It's actually a perfect day for an outside wedding. The shade is just slightly dappled with sunlight, so it's not too hot or too bright, and the wind is swirling, so there's sometimes a rustling of leaves, and even the bigger branches of the oaks sort of musically sway. There are about fifty people here, some doctors I recognize, some grateful patients of C. H. who introduce themselves and tell me what a wonderful man he is. There are waiters going around with champagne, and I drink two glasses quickly, which make it easier for me to chitchat when I meet two of Destiny's friends, who look New Agey but not too New Agey, dressed in earth tones and floppy hats, wearing very little makeup, plain but sort of pretty.

There are red and pink rose petals scattered all down the center aisle and up to the Oriental rug that's spread on the ground between the candelabras for the altar, and when Destiny's Unitarian minister, a woman in a long white robe with a fringed strip of colorful brocade hanging around her neck, steps up to the rug and calls everyone to take a seat, I take one more glass of champagne from a waiter and head up the center aisle to the front row of the groom's side, where Destiny said she wanted C. H.'s family to sit, but neither of C. H.'s sisters who just live in

Little Rock, nor Uncle John, of course, who's busy being a senator, bothered to come, so I'm alone in the row, but not feeling lonely or even dreading the ceremony. I'm actually looking forward to hearing the vows that Destiny and C. H. wrote themselves and have kept secret from each other.

When the string trio—a violin, a viola, and a cello—begins to play, the wedding party enters in a procession from the sides, first C. H. and Dwane and Paul from the right, with C. H. and Dwane wearing identical navy sport coats and red silk ties and khakis and rolling their shoulders trying to get comfortable, while Paul, although in a business suit, already looks comfortable, then from the left Destiny comes in wearing a pale pink suit, then Rain and Whitney, both in pale blue strapless dresses, and once everybody's in position, with Destiny and C. H. standing on the Oriental rug, the minister leads a kind of typical ceremony, with a prayer followed by a song and a statement about marriage, and I start thinking about my own love life, about how I've never had a real relationship. The closest I've come was with Brinson, and now that's completely over, hardly even a friendship. I don't believe I'll ever get married, and it's something I've accepted, though every once in a while, like when I'm riding alone in a cab after seeing a really wonderful play, I think it might be nice.

Dwane goes into his sport coat for the rings to give C. H., who then gives them to the minister. Then the minister tells us that C. H. and Destiny have written their own vows, and she looks at C. H., then C. H. looks at Destiny, and I lean forward to hear every word.

"I love you, Destiny," he says, "and, well, I'm proud to be marrying you."

Paul catches my eye, and we give each other a look.

The minister turns to Destiny, who is gazing at C. H. in an unblinking way, like she's awestruck by what he just said and has completely forgotten whatever it was that she came up with in her writing room. But then, in a whisper, she begins.

"C. H.," she says, "do you know what I've learned to stop listening to?" C. H. shakes his head like the question is not rhetorical, and a smile breaks across the minister's face. Then Destiny says, her voice growing louder, "To blood. The true bond of love and family is never shared through blood but through air. Through the space between us that unites us. And I vow I will always listen, C. H., from this day forward, to the aura of love and family that is ours."

The minister nods and says, "Very nice." And with the authority vested in her by the state of Arkansas, she pronounces them husband and wife, then tells C. H. to kiss his bride.

The string trio begins playing, then the wedding party files down the center aisle, and I turn back to watch them, and I see Hardscrabble employees, in their red jackets with the crest on the pocket, waiting by the line of golf carts, waiting to take us to the clubhouse, where the reception room with the dark rose carpet and lighter rose walls will be decorated with candles and lilies and maidenhair ferns, where I'll walk through the heavy double-doors and throw a coin in the fountain, where I'll walk on the white marble floor through the Hall of Presidents and see the black-and-white portraits of Chandler's father and grandfather and think of Chandler and all that has happened to her, think of our history there, of all our time on the tennis courts, of all the lunch tickets signed with short yellow pencils, of all that we have together that is not blood.

A Secret Word

Chandler

During the week, when everyone else is at work, I like to go to the Riverside Park tennis courts and practice my serve on the red clay, and after, I lie out on the grass on a hill, so that when I lift my head, I'm able to see the Hudson River, and in the distance, across the water, New Jersey. My schedule at Deutsche Bank, where I work now, is flexible. I work weekends and only an occasional weekday. But I used to be a lawyer, and sometimes midday in midtown, wearing an uncomfortable skirt with hose and heels, grabbing lunch to take up to my desk, I'd see someone like I am now, dressed in shorts and a tank top, holding a racquet, her ponytail swinging as she bounded down the stairs to the subway.

I'm walking down the promenade, and the wind is watering my eyes as I look at the river, at how the sun hits the current, and when I'm close enough to the courts, I can see that only one person is there, a man I think, practicing his serve.

There is an air of elegance at Riverside, even though they are public courts. They are always swept clean, and there are little pots of pansies and begonias set around, and the guy that runs things is very thin with silver hair, and he looks like he might have run a tennis club in Monte Carlo before he decided to settle down with his family on the Upper West Side of Manhattan and work here, lazily but with dignity.

I sign in, writing down my permit number, and go to a court in the middle, far enough away from the man practicing his serve, so as not to bother him, but close enough in case he might want to play. He looks cute and relatively young, around thirty, a little older than I am, with black hair and a build like Andre Agassi's. I stretch on the court and watch him, and his serve is terrible. Kind of like how old women do, he doesn't turn his side to the net, and he doesn't take a full swing. He just sort of tosses the ball and slaps at it, then he gets frustrated when it doesn't have any power and slings his racquet across the court and turns and sees me and looks horribly embarrassed. "My God," he says in a southern drawl, "I'm sorry. I didn't know anyone else was out here."

I smile. "It's all right."

He goes to retrieve his racquet, and I get out two cans of balls from my canvas bag, which also holds a towel for lying out on later, and start hitting my serve, or not hitting it rather because it's windy and I have a terrible toss anyway, and it gets even worse when I'm nervous and think someone's watching me. Finally my toss works and I hit it hard down the middle of the box, and I look up, hoping the man saw it, but he's not watching. He's dropping the ball and practicing his backhand, and it's an awful thing, too, sometimes one-handed, other times two-handed.

I don't know how I muster the courage to go up to him. Lately I've been like that. Talking more to people at work, going to parties. I've even gone on a few fix-up dates, meeting for a drink or dinner.

"Would you like to hit?" I say.

"You mean play a game?" he says. He really has a southern voice, and a nice, soft one that's more genteel than twang.

"Just hit it back and forth," I say, "no keeping score or serving or anything."

He smiles. "Yeah, sure." He holds out his hand. "I'm Mark Starling."

"Chandler," I say and shake his hand.

We begin hitting, and he's doing all right, getting most shots back, all the while saying, "My God, you're good. You're like a pro."

"I used to be number one in Arkansas," I say. "When I was a kid."

"Really?" he says, walking up to the net to collect the balls. "You're from Arkansas? You don't have an accent that I can hear."

"Well, not like yours," I say and stroll up to the net, so we don't have to yell.

"Do I have an accent?" he says.

I start laughing.

"What?" he says. "Is it that thick?"

I'm still laughing, and I can't stop. I feel all giddy about him, already. He has this sweet smile, and dark, intense eyes.

"Are you always off on Fridays, Campbell?" he says. But he says *Fri-dees*. "All the publishing people get off on Fri-dees, I'm learning."

I smile. "It's *Chandler*."

"My Lord," he says, "I'm sorry, Chandler."

"I work tonight," I say. "Then all day Saturday and Sunday. I'm a proofreader at an investment bank." Mindlessly, I flip my racquet and catch it on the grip, real nonchalantly, the way I did sometimes before a match, or at match point, when I was thirteen, to prove to my opponents I was unintimidated.

"Wow, you're off all week," he says. "What a great job." He bends down to pick up the last ball. "Those are strange hours, though."

"Yeah," I say. "So you're in publishing?"

He shrugs. "Sort of. I'm a writer just getting published." He looks away, shyly, like he's not used to talking about himself or bragging. "That's why I'm here in New York, to meet my editor."

"So you just got a book deal?" I ask, and he nods, walking up to the net cradling all six balls. "Is it fiction or something else?"

"A novel," he says. *"Drowning on Dry Land."*

"Wow, that's a great title. I got my bachelor's degree in English," I say, and I can't believe I just said that.

He laughs and holds out the balls to me. "You take them. I'm no good starting things off."

"Oh, you're doing all right." I take three of them and look up, and he's smiling at me.

"Chandler, you have the prettiest smile in New York City."

Of course, I smile again. "Thanks," I say. "So what do you do when you're not in New York visiting your editor?"

"I teach ninth- and tenth-grade world literature at a prep school in Mobile, Alabama. It's not as glamorous as it sounds."

"But you're off all summer though, right?" I say. "Not just on Fri-dees."

"Yeah," he says, "but I'm only visiting for a few days, not the whole summer. I fly back tomorrow."

"Oh," I say. "I was hoping we'd get to play tennis again." I turn around and walk back to the baseline.

We hit awhile longer, until Mark says he has to stop, that he's not in the best shape. And I'm not either, but I'm trying not to breathe too hard. I'm standing up straight, not slumping like I sometimes do after exercising.

On the walk out, we stop at the water fountain, and I motion for Mark to go first, and as he takes a long drink, I let my hair down out of the ponytail. I think I may look better that way, more like a girl and not a tennis player. Then when I take a drink, my hair falls in front of my face, getting wet a little, and Mark holds it back for me, and I feel a shock when he touches the back of my neck. I turn around, and he's looking at me with those dark brown eyes, and I feel a bit off-guard, and I step away from him.

"You really are pretty, Chandler," he says. "You're the prettiest girl in New York City."

I clutch my bag under my arm. "I don't know about that."

Mark smiles. "Would you like to sit down for a minute? Cool off and talk?"

"Okay," I say and open my bag. "I even have a towel."

We walk onto the grass, under a cluster of trees, and I spread out the towel, and look about twenty yards down at some other people who are lying in the sun, two teenage girls in bikinis, a couple who's been biking in T-shirts and shorts, and now Mark and I sit cross-legged on my green towel in the shade, our tennis racquets beside us.

"So," he says, "how'd you end up in New York?"

I tell him how I went to law school at NYU and was a lawyer for about six months, but hated it and quit, then how I started proofreading for Deutsche Bank.

"I took German in college," he says. "I'm not any good at it, though. And I thought about going to law school, whenever the writing wasn't going so well. I'm glad I stuck with it. My novel will be out in just a mere year and a half."

"Drowning on Dry Land," I say.

He smiles, looking impressed with my memory. "I could send you a galley when it comes out, if you want to read it early."

"I'd love that," I say. "I've never known a writer who actually has a book coming out. I work with a lot of them proofreading, but they're all still struggling." My hair keeps blowing in my eyes, and I have to use both hands to hold it back. He runs a hand through his hair, even though it's short and the wind doesn't move it much.

"Would you want to give me your address?" he asks.

"All right." I reach into my bag and find a pen, but nothing to write on, so he gives me his agent's card, which is from ICM, and I've heard of that, and I write my name and address on the back of the card and hand it to him.

"Thanks, Chandler," he says, looking at what I've written, and I'm hoping he didn't forget my name again. "Could you give me your phone number, too?" he says. "Sometimes, after I've been out drinking late at night, I like to call pretty girls in New York City."

I laugh and take the card from him and write down my number.

• • •

That night at work, as I turn pages of a pitch book, trying to make sense of a banker's handwriting, marking red corrections to words and numbers, I think about Mark Starling and Mobile, Alabama.

I walk over to the map of the United States on the wall, which is under the world map that I often look at to double-check spellings of cities and countries, and outline with my finger the black letters of *Mobile,* the Deep South, with antebellum homes and live oaks and Spanish moss, and wonder if I will ever go there.

• • •

On Monday, like I do every Monday after working all weekend, I call the deli on the corner and order three 20-ounce Cokes, two cups of ice, and two large Evians. Then I look at the Coffee Shop menu I know by heart, so I can order enough food to last all day. Today I decide on quesadillas for lunch, and meat loaf and mashed potatoes for dinner. I call and place my order, and the guy who answers for deliveries knows my voice and says, "26 Gramercy, right?" which is my address, then he says, "Used to be 35 East Tenth," which is my old address, and he laughs. I say,

"Yes, that's right," and only laugh a polite laugh because I've heard this joke a million times.

The phone rings right back, and I think it's the Coffee Shop guy telling me the quesadilla is no longer chicken but ham, and he knows I don't like the ham, but after I say hello, it's a southern voice, Mark Starling's.

"Hi there, Campbell," he says.

"It's Chandler," I say, but I know he knows. "Are you drinking already?" I say. "In the afternoon?"

"You know I am," he says and laughs. "Do you miss me?"

And before I can stop myself, I say, "I do. I really do."

I hear my buzzer, and it's so loud that Mark can hear it, too. I tell him it's the deli with my Cokes and ice and water, and he says, "You have to order ice and water?"

"I don't have much of a freezer on my little refrigerator," I tell him, "and the water from the faucet sometimes comes out brown." I buzz in the delivery guy and wait by the door. "Mark, can I call you back?" I say and grab a pen and paper. He gives me his number, and I feel a thrill writing it down, and I'm smiling so much when the deli guy appears, and he smiles back at me, and I tip him three dollars, and he thanks me several times, and I wish I had even more to give him, at least a five, because he's always so happy, and even though I've never talked to him because he doesn't speak English very well, I can tell he is a nice and wonderful person.

I'm nervous to call Mark back, so I wait until evening, but when we do talk, we talk easily and for hours. I tell him about my father, how he killed himself and why. I tell Mark how much I loved my father, and that sometimes I'm mad at him, but mostly I'm grateful to have had him as a father for twenty-four years. And Mark listens to me. He doesn't tell me about someone he knew who killed himself or about his grandmother who died or about any tragedy that's ever happened to him. He just lets me talk, lets me tell him everything I want to tell him, doesn't take anything away from my tragedy by telling me one of his own. He just listens.

The next night Mark calls again, and he tells me about his family. His parents are divorced, but he says they're better off. He has a brother that he gets along with well. He has two dogs, but doesn't hunt, and I'm relieved because my father hunted, and sometimes I would come home and see him cleaning quail, seated on a lawn chair in the garage, with a knife working through the feathers, and I would feel sad.

Mark and I talk the rest of the week, and I even give him my number at Deutsche Bank, and on the weekend, he calls me there, and my proofreader friends kid me about his accent, and they even catch me touching Mobile on the map and say, "Dreaming about the South again, Chandler?" I never thought I would want to leave New York, and now my dream is to live in Alabama.

I get a card in the mail from him. It's a pink card with a small red heart on the outside, and inside he writes the lyrics to one of my favorite songs, "Responsible," by one of my favorite singers, Brinson Carr.

> But I want somebody to lie.
> And release me into the past.
> And I want to know what I knew.
> For a secret word to tell you that I know I'm not responsible.

And I start to cry because I used to listen to that song over and over after my father died. And I would wonder, How is a word told but still secret, and what is the word exactly, and is it different for each of us? And how can a lie even lead you to this word of truth, to solve your worst problem? Of course, what I really wanted to know was, How could my father be the perfect father and also be the cruelest? How could he be so responsible and so irresponsible? How could I, how could we all, be so responsible and so irresponsible? Listening to that song was like reading a Hindu hymn. I eventually had to acknowledge the contradictions and embrace them. I had to stop listening to the words and thinking of words and begin to feel the music that was playing.

I've been tempted to ask Brinson about the meaning of his lyrics, but it's always seemed inappropriate or impolite because the song might be as personal and private for him as it is for me, and if it's not, if the words were tossed in randomly for their beat, I don't want to know. I'm not sure if I ever mentioned any of this to Mark, but when we were talking about music, I did tell him Brinson Carr was someone I knew, someone who used to date my best friend, but Mark said he didn't know who Brinson was. Mark must have gone out and bought Brinson's CD. He must hear and remember everything I say. He must hear more than I realize.

Evan would have never done anything like that for me. Nobody I've gone out with has ever done anything like that for me. Not even Mitchell, and I was engaged to him. The closest anyone came was when Scott Foster sent me a letter after my father died containing a quote from Aeschylus about suffering that I saw taped to his office, a quote I like, but a quote I'm certain he has given to many girls, with or without dead fathers.

I call Mark right away and thank him for the card, telling him it was a wonderful surprise, that I never get any real mail. And he says he has another surprise for me. That he's coming to New York on my birthday over Labor Day weekend, if it's all right with me. "Of course, it's all right," I say. Then I realize that I've only spent one afternoon with him, and he will be in my two-room apartment for three nights. That, I guess, he will be sleeping in bed with me, and we haven't even kissed. "I can't wait," I say.

* * *

I don't talk to Sarah as much as I used to because she now has an agent from the Gersh Agency, which she says is pretty good, and has been going on more auditions, and to a voice coach twice a week, and three nights a week she practices with a punk band.

And I also don't see her because she bought a dog, a golden retriever named Clover, but she pronounces it *Clovière,* like Molière. And every morning before her day of auditioning and singing begins, she takes the dog to a dog spa in Chelsea. I didn't even know there was such a place, but there are lots of them.

On my birthday weekend, this weekend, Sarah's going to stay at the SoHo Grand Hotel, just to get away, she says. Apparently it's a very dog-friendly hotel where the bellboys carry dog treats, and there's even a doggie room-service menu. I've told Sarah all about Mark, and she wants us to meet her at the hotel bar to celebrate, everything on her, and Mark and I have arranged for a writer friend of his to meet us there, too, sort of a blind date for Sarah.

* * *

I'm waiting on my bed dressed all in black, hoping I look thin, watching channel 77 on television, which is the channel that's hooked up to the video surveillance in the lobby. When I first moved in here, I used to watch people coming in and out of the building for hours. Now I'm watching the doorman pace back and forth.

To prepare for Mark's arrival, I ordered a maid from the phone book, and it only cost forty dollars, and it was well worth it because the place looks spotless. I also bought new white pajamas from Macy's that I think are sexy, but not too much like I'm trying to be sexy.

Finally I see Mark Starling, dressed neatly in an oxford and jeans, and he's talking to the doorman and looking for my name on the list of names and apartment numbers inside the first door, then I hear a buzz in my apartment. I get up, trying to stay calm, and go to push the talk button on my intercom. "Come on up," I say, "sixth floor." I hurry to the bathroom to make sure my makeup is okay, then out to the hall to wait for him.

"Hi there," I say, as he steps out of the elevator. I look at him a moment, but he doesn't say anything. He just looks at me, up and down, like he's trying to match my voice on the telephone to my appearance, which I hope he hasn't forgotten over this past month and isn't disappointed in, and says, "God, you're beautiful. Happy birthday!"

"Thanks," I say, feeling awkward. "Come in." I motion with my arm for him to go first, and as he's walking ahead of me, I notice he's wearing Wrangler jeans.

I don't know how he knows I've noticed, but he says, "Do you like my Wrangler's?"

I smile. "I haven't seen anyone wear them in a long time."

"You haven't?" he says. "I think they look pretty good."

"Me, too," I say.

"So," he says, setting his bag down, then opening his arms.

I move to hug him, tentatively at first, then hold him tightly, and our bodies feel perfect together.

When he lets go of me, he says, "That, Chandler, was the best hug I've ever had."

It's almost eight, and I can just picture Sarah and Clover sitting in the SoHo Grand bar waiting for us. "Do you mind if we go ahead and go?" I say.

"Yeah, sure," he says. "But do you mind if I brush my teeth?"

"Oh, no," I say. "Go ahead."

He reaches into his bag and pulls out his shaving kit and goes into the bathroom. He leaves the door slightly open, and I can see him brushing his teeth, then washing his face and patting dry with one of my towels. It feels so nice and strange at the same time having him here.

Outside, Mark says how beautiful Gramercy Park is, and I tell him it's the only private park in New York, that you need a key to go in.

"Let's go in for a second," he says.

"Well, I don't have a key myself," I tell him. "We'd have to go back and get it from the doorman."

"Mohammed?" Mark says. "I introduced myself."

I smile, thinking about how my mother also introduced herself to Mohammed.

We walk to Third Avenue, and it's softly raining, and Mark asks if we need to go back for an umbrella, but I say, "Nah," and he smiles. I hold my arm out, and I think Mark is impressed with my cab-hailing ability because I'm able to get a cab ahead of two couples who are across the street.

He looks a little confused and taken aback when I open the door myself and get in. "Three-ten West Broadway," I tell the driver, "between Grand and Canal."

In the cab, we don't sit close, and I'm wondering if he wants to move closer, to rest his hand on my leg, to lace his fingers with mine, but he doesn't do any of that. He keeps glancing back and forth with his intense, brown eyes, from the window and the city lights, to me in the shadow.

Mark pays for the taxi, and this makes me feel good, like it's a real first date, then says, "This is cool," as he opens the door for me to the hotel. To get to the lobby and bar, we walk up these freight-like steel stairs, which are illuminated from below, and everything seems to be gray and black and brown, and I feel like this was the right place to bring Mark, and I feel grateful to Sarah for giving us something to do on Mark's first night here.

Even though it's crowded and the lights are dim, it's not hard to spot Sarah and Clover on a couch. Clover is wearing a new rhinestone collar, and in her mouth is a ball that flashes a red light, while Sarah is wearing a floppy, shiny black hat. She sees us and stands up and waves, and now I see that her hair is brown. I give her a hug, and she says, "Happy birthday," and I introduce her to Mark, and she shakes his hand.

"Hi, Sarah," he says in his long drawn-out way. "I'm so happy to meet you."

She smiles. "Hi," she says, speaking real southern. "I've heard all about you." Then she winks at me and lifts Clover's paw and has Mark shake it.

"You changed your hair?" I say. Last month I was thinking of coloring my hair darker, and Sarah held Clover's mouth and moved it like a human's, saying, "Come on, Chandler, do you want to be brown like Rain and Whitney and Destiny, or do you want to be blonde, like me and Clovière?"

Sarah smiles. "I think it's more *me*. I've been hiding behind that blonde hair for too long."

Mark doesn't know what to say. He pauses a moment, then says, "Well, I love your hat."

"It's a rain hat," Sarah says. "Everyone in this city ought to have one. I hate walking down the sidewalk and getting poked by everyone's giant umbrella."

Mark and I sit down on a couch opposite Sarah and Clover, and a waitress comes over and asks if we need anything.

"Get a Tartini," Sarah says. "Three Tartinis," Sarah says.

"What's that?" Mark asks.

The waitress tells us it's a martini with Stoli raspberry, Chambord, and cranberry juice.

"And lemon juice," Sarah adds. "And could I have some water for my dog, please?"

The waitress is model tall and thin and doesn't seem all too thrilled to be waiting on us.

187

"And could we have some champagne?" Sarah says and points to me. "It's her birthday."

"What kind?" the waitress asks.

Sarah thinks a moment and smiles. "Give us your least expensive bottle of Dom Perignon."

• • •

When Mark's friend Tom arrives, we're all pretty tipsy from our Tartinis and champagne, and Clover is asleep on the floor next to a silver bowl of water. Mark stands up, unsteady on his feet, and shakes Tom's hand, and introduces Sarah and me. Tom's an athletic, square-shouldered guy who is still hip-looking enough for Sarah to like, I think, with his spiked blond hair and goatee. He sits down next to Sarah, and she asks the waitress to bring another champagne glass for Tom and orders another round of Tartinis.

"You're drunk, man," Tom says, looking at Mark. "I've never seen you this drunk."

"I'm fine," Mark says, and puts his hand on my leg, and he whispers to me, "I don't know if I can afford all this."

"It's okay," I say. "Sarah's paying for it."

"Oh, she can't do that," Mark tries to whisper, but Sarah hears him.

"I've got it, Mark. For Chandler's birthday. This is her present."

"Well," Mark says, "thank you, Sarah."

Tom takes his first drink of Tartini. "This is strong."

Mark gets up to go to the bathroom and almost falls. He looks at me, and I smile. "Lord, you have a pretty smile," he says.

"What about me?" Sarah says and smiles really big and squints her eyes, the same way I used to do as a kid when I'd have my picture taken.

"Yours is pretty," Mark says, "but nobody's is as pretty as Chandler's."

"Ahhh," Tom says, and Sarah laughs.

As soon as Mark's out of sight, Tom starts going on about how much Mark likes me. That after he met me on the tennis court, he couldn't stop talking about me.

"I play tennis, Tom," Sarah says.

"You do?" he says.

"I used to be great," she says, leaning back, almost lying down on the couch.

"You were?" he says and sinks back next to her, and they begin to talk softly to each other, and Clover jumps up next to me, and I pet her and finish off my second Tartini.

"Excuse me," I say, but they don't hear me, and I get up.

In the bathroom, there are other girls, taller and thinner and prettier, primping, but when I look in the mirror I feel different from how I normally feel around these kinds of women. I feel like I can compete.

I decide to go to the men's bathroom to check on Mark. I walk to the entrance and yell, "Mark. Mark Starling, author extraordinaire," but nobody answers.

I go back to where we're sitting, but it's just Tom there, and he tells me that Sarah has taken Clover to the room, that Clover's pretty worn out from all the action.

"Where's Mark?" Tom asks.

"I don't know," I say. "I thought the bathroom."

"I'll go look," he says.

I'm starting to feel kind of spinny because I haven't eaten much today, not really much in the last few days, trying to lose five pounds before Mark arrived. I lean back and close my eyes a few minutes. When I look up, I see skinny, perfect Sarah, still wearing her rain hat, coming toward me.

"Mark's really drunk," she says. "Tom took him up to the room with Clovière. I don't think he really drinks."

"Is he okay?" I ask.

"Just an occasional *Budweiser*," she says in a country accent. "I'm kidding," she says. "He's fine. Just drunk. I think he's wonderful. And he's in love with you."

"How can you tell?" I ask.

"I can just tell," she says. "And Tom told me."

"Let's go up," I say.

• • •

"Death by mini-bar," Sarah says as we enter the room. Tom's already there mixing two vodka tonics for Sarah and him.

"I just want a Coke," I say. "And pretzels."

I sit on the bed next to Mark, and I'm charmed watching him sleep, with Clover's red ball flashing under his chin. I take the ball and throw it down to Clover, and she nudges it with her nose, lets it roll, then catches it with her mouth.

Tom hands me a Coke, and it tastes great, much better than a Tartini, and I feel like I'm starving and start eating the pretzels, one after another, until I feel Mark grab my elbow, smiling, his eyes barely open. "You look sexy all in black drinking that Coke and eating those pretzels."

"I do?" I say.

He nods and closes his eyes again, and I'm suddenly afraid that something could be really wrong with him, that he might not ever wake up. I've been like this many times, afraid if the phone rings late at night that my mother is dead, or if Sarah's late meeting me somewhere that she's had a heart attack or has killed herself. "Get up," I say and softly run my hand down his face, and he flinches. "Please," I say, grabbing his shoulder, "please, please, please wake up."

He opens his eyes and reaches out and touches my hair. "You have the softest hair," he says.

"The softest hair in New York City?" I say.

"No," he says, beginning to sit up, "the softest hair." He

shakes his head, then gently holds my face in his hands. "Please, forgive me."

"What for?"

"I shouldn't have drunk so much on my flight here. I'm a little scared of you, I guess. Of falling in love. Of disappointing you. Of embarrassing myself."

I take his face in my hands the way he's still holding mine. I shake my head, and before I can speak, as if he knows what I'm about to say, he shakes his head, too, and we're now rocking, locked in each other's grasp, smiling and shaking our heads, then nodding, as if to questions and declarations in a language we have just discovered and is all our own.

A Not Yet Shattered Bliss

Leigh

I've had my money clenched in my hand since I saw the signs for the toll booths ahead, I'm just a bridge away now, and I have never crossed a toll bridge before. I've got exact change, two dollars, so I pass right through, and the road immediately rises, as if over a hill, and then it levels, and I see that this is already the bridge, and before me is the widest water I have ever seen, wider than the Mississippi River I crossed yesterday or Mobile Bay I crossed this morning, and the water's rough and beautiful and dark green, and beyond all the water in the distance far in front of me is the flat white land I have so long dreamed of. The sun flashes in and out of gray and white clouds, and I begin to cry and laugh at once, thinking that all I have left in this world and all I need are with me in this Honda, except for my mother, and I miss her, but only for the moment. I can't help wishing she could see me now, could see Destin now, then hurry away.

I left everything to Cassidy. The apartment, the furniture, even the pots and pans. I only wanted my clothes and my car, a box of keepsakes, a divorce that was amicable, and an opportunity to live on my own.

I'm riding into Destin with enough money saved to live on

192

for about a month, the only time I've ever needed between jobs to find another. It'll be cheap motels until I find a cheap apartment with a pool, but for tonight and tonight only I've got a reservation at Embassy Suites. A Celebration Suite, with a four-poster bed, a jacuzzi, and an ocean view. And there's even access to a private beach.

. . .

Chandler

I've been here a year now, since last December, when everyone thought I was crazy for leaving Manhattan and moving to Fairhope, a pretty little resort town on the eastern shore of Alabama that Mark thought I'd like better than Mobile. I'm still not completely used to driving. Since I don't work anywhere, only at home helping to edit Mark's next book (his first book doesn't come out for another two months), I never go very far.

I'm driving now where I always drive, along Mobile Bay, past live oaks and Spanish moss, down the hill to the fishing pier and small marina, where you can always hear the wind knocking the rigging against the masts of the docked sailboats, and instead of looping around the fountain and the flag pole, I take the side road to the public beach, then park by the duck pond. I love to watch these certain three adult white ducks strut along the road to guard the younger ducks, sometimes blocking the road, as they stretch out their necks and flap their wings and hiss at people. Sometimes they even venture out of the pond to the beach and then to the bay with the seagulls and pelicans.

I still feel a little guilty being relieved to be here and not in Manhattan. On September 11, when Mark called me from work on his break, like he does every day, he hadn't yet heard about the planes flying into the Twin Towers, then while I was telling him, I watched the first tower collapse, and I screamed and we cried and couldn't believe it. He finally didn't know what to say, except how grateful he was that I wasn't in New York anymore, and I felt defensive, saying that I never worked on Tuesday, that I would've been home in my apartment, probably asleep. And then I began to think of all the people I knew who did work on Tuesday. I began to think of all the people I saw getting off the subway in the World Trade Center who worked there every day. I thought of Deutsche Bank, of the pizza place down the street, of the Amish Market next door, and I knew that they would be covered in debris and ash and soot, or gone.

When the second tower fell, I looked for people I knew running for their lives down Liberty Street, and I called a proofreading friend, an actress, who had moved to Los Angeles the same time I moved here, and we felt helpless, not knowing if anyone we knew had died. She had tried to get through to Manhattan, but all the lines were busy, and I had tried to call Sarah, and I knew she wouldn't have been down there, but I just needed to hear her voice.

I get out of the car, and even though it's winter, it's still warm, and it's shocking to be here, walking along this small beach, looking at the brown but beautiful water of the bay, with the city of Mobile in the distance, where Mark is teaching and I hope is always safe. We've been married for six months now, after a small ceremony in Sewanee, Tennessee, at the Natural Land Bridge, because I remembered going there as a kid with my father and being surrounded by trees and looking down on valleys and feeling like we were the only ones who lived in the world. And then Mark and I went on our honeymoon in Italy, first in Venice, then in Florence, even staying two nights at the Grand Hotel Villa Cora.

· · · ·

Sarah

Don't look, I tell myself as I walk past University Street, not wanting to see the empty space in the skyline where the Twin Towers used to stand. I know it would be even worse where I used to live on MacDougal Street because I would use the towers for direction whenever I'd get confused walking through SoHo or the West Village, coming out of the Bleecker Street subway.

Every time I walk through Union Square Park, which is near where I live now, I think about that day when I saw people running uptown covered in ash. I was in my apartment sleeping when I got a call from my friend Adam, and he told me the news. I threw on some clothes, grabbed my video camera, and from University Street was able to film the second tower falling. I remember walking back home through the park that looked so green and seeing college students, I think from the NYU dorms that are right there, swinging each other around, dressed like bohemians and acting like kids let out of school early for snow, and I wanted to shake them, didn't they realize what had happened, while others, those who had escaped the towers, with only their eyes and mouths wiped clean, waited at the bus stop. I videotaped it all, and I felt wrong doing it but also right and kept on, videotaping all those deaths and near-deaths, documenting them, trying to connect with the tragedy in my only way.

I taped people sitting outside at the Coffee Shop eating like it was a typical sunny day, and I taped a large group gathered around a fruit stand on Seventeenth Street, because behind the fruit stand was an open van with a small television blaring news.

I didn't know anyone who died. Not even a friend of a friend who died. And though I feel sad, thinking of all the sadness all around me, mostly I feel gratitude, for my life, and for my friends and family, and for Clover.

. . .

Leigh

It takes me three tries before I figure out how to use the key card and get the green light to open my door. And I'm amazed at what I see. There are two rooms to my Celebration Suite, and each has its own television. Plus there's a desk and a couch and a mini-fridge and a microwave, and there's a snack tray with gourmet coffee and popcorn and Famous Amos cookies. I drop my bags and hurry to the bed, and it's a four-poster like it's supposed to be, with posts nearly reaching the ceiling. And neatly folded on the foot of the bed are two white robes, one I'll wear tonight and one for the morning. I turn around and check out the closet, and I find an iron and an ironing board and a safe for valuables, which makes me giddy at first, then sort of sad that I have nothing to put in it. Then I go to the window and draw the curtains to see if I really do have an ocean view, and there it is, across the street and between the condos, the foaming aqua-green surf, and it is gorgeous.

I smile until I can smile no longer and reach to open the window for air, but there isn't a way to open it. Then I remember that the room comes with a jacuzzi, and I head for the bathroom to have a look. I'm disappointed. I was expecting one I could stretch out in completely, and this jacuzzi looks no bigger than a tub, or not much bigger.

I decide to test the size and step in, not bothering to take off my shoes or any of my clothes, and I lie down, and I can't believe that my shoes don't even touch the other side. There's plenty of room in here for two of me. I'm realizing that a person could live a lifetime in a Celebration Suite.

I rest my head back and imagine what it will feel like when the jacuzzi is full and I am undressed and the air is rushing through hot water.

• • •

Chandler

Mark will be home soon. This afternoon, we'll be driving to New Orleans to see Brinson Carr. I've reserved a room at the Hampton Inn in the Garden District, and tomorrow Mark is going to call in sick. I'm so excited to see Brinson again. Just to be back in a bar drinking, listening to live music, seems exciting. Brinson is playing at Carrollton Station, and from what I can tell from the Internet, it's next to an old train station and is a pretty cool place, with hardwood floors and church pews for seats.

I've really gotten Mark hooked on Brinson's music, and I know that when we see him Brinson will be nice, but I have this crazy insecure feeling that he won't remember me when he sees me outside of New York. That somehow being married and living in Alabama have changed my look altogether.

I'm sitting on the living-room floor next to our CD player, and when I hear Mark pull up, I press Play, and Brinson's music comes out blaring. I greet Mark at the door, and we kiss a long kiss, and he says, "All right, we're going to New Orleans!" Then we start dancing to Brinson's music, and we're not very good, but we do this often because it's fun that we're so bad and because we've finally gotten to the point where Mark is able to turn me without getting us tangled.

I'm already packed, so Mark just throws clean boxers, jeans, a shirt, and his shaving kit into my bag, and we grab our leather jackets we bought in Florence, and we're out the door.

As we travel over the sloughs of south Mississippi, past the cranes at the shipyards in the distance, past billboards for the Biloxi casinos and billboards for the New Orleans casinos, we listen to Brinson's music and sing.

This will be our first time to go to the Garden District. Last year, we went to the French Quarter for a day during Mardi Gras, and it was fun to fight the crowds for beads and later hang our catch all over the house, from lamps and doorknobs and bedposts, but I'm not sure I'll ever want to go back.

• • •

Sarah

I just got back from an open-call audition, and I'm sitting on the kitchen floor, feeling exhausted and defeated, and eating delivery from the Coffee Shop with Clover. I'm having chicken tamales, and she's having apple pie à la mode. From now on I'm sticking with private auditions that either my agent has set up or I've set up myself. "Isn't that right, Clover?" I say, and I pet her. I've always wanted to be in a Woody Allen movie, but waiting in a line with a million other people just was not worth it.

I got lucky finding an agent because when I performed my thesis at Circle in the Square, a really good one was there watching, and she liked me and my friend Shawn and signed us both. Shawn is out in Los Angeles right now on a successful show, and I'm not jealous or anything, and that surprises me a little. There's even a website about him, and he's been interviewed by several teen magazines and is becoming something of a heartthrob.

I haven't had a big break like that, even though I did finally get my SAG card, but I'm kind of bummed out that I can't do any nonunion work and was really bummed out when the strike was going on. But it may have been good for me because that's when I started singing more, and now my band plays at the Elbow Room about twice a month. It's really a rock band, but I like to call it a punk band because I think that sounds cooler.

And tonight, for the first time ever, we're playing at Lakeside Lounge. God, I wish Chandler were here to see me.

• • •

Leigh

Standing with my arms at my side and letting the ocean wind whip my sleeves and hair, I take deep breaths, one after the other, until I am light-headed with calm. This salt air is medicine to me, and I am now certain that I will become who I really am here, to be cured of all that I never was. I know from my travel brochures that the Atlantic and the Caribbean and all the coastal rivers eventually cycle here and wash against this shore, though the Destin sand remains perfectly clean and white and packed smooth, littered only with an occasional brown pelican feather.

I check my watch and start heading back across the boardwalk to the hotel. It's four o'clock, and in an hour, from five to seven, the bar will start offering free cocktails and snacks.

I turn the air down low in my room and soak in the jacuzzi until I'm so comfortable that I almost don't feel the bones in my body. I'm a little nervous to go down to the bar alone. I don't think I've ever even been in a bar without Cassidy. I'm thirty-one years old, and I think it's about time I do things on my own.

I need to get out to cool off and move around and feel human again, but before I do I turn on the shower, and standing up, I wash my hair with the Embassy Suites shampoo. Then I dry off with a thick white towel and put on the Embassy Suites lotion and wear one of the robes as I apply my makeup. I dry my hair with the hotel's hair dryer, even though it's not very powerful, because I just want to use everything they offer here.

I'm not sure if where the cocktails are is dressy or casual, so I iron my gray pants and black blouse, and when I look at myself in the full-length mirror, I think I look fine, and I'll be dressed appropriately no matter what anyone else is wearing.

From the glass elevator, I look out into the garden atrium, and on the other side of a maze of palm trees and bamboo and day lillies, woven with walkways lined with old-fashioned street lamps, I see the bar, called Calypso Café.

I follow one of the walkways and stop at the fountain in the center of the atrium to find a penny in my purse and make a wish. A statue of a woman in a long revealing gown stands with a leg bent and a hip swaying in the middle of the fountain, with her eyes closed, it seems, in a moment of quiet confidence. *To be you,* I think, and toss two pennies at her feet.

I guess I'm looking around like I don't know what I'm doing because a man in an airbrushed sweatshirt tells me you have to walk up to the bar to get your free drinks. "Oh, right," I say and smile. I begin to make my way there, and I notice four men dressed nicely in starched oxford shirts and slacks, and I try not to look at them as I pass, but I slow my step and listen to them because they're British. They're talking so proper, like they're having cocktails in the garden of their country house, and I've never heard anyone speak like this except on television, and then I see that one of them notices me, that he's looking at me, at all of me, and I suddenly feel like the whole world is possible in this hotel, in Destin, in Florida, in London, in who knows where my life will take me.

· · ·

Chandler

The Hampton Inn in the Garden District isn't like the Hampton Inns you see on the highway. It's like a hotel you might see in Italy, with a marble floor and a garden with fountains. Mark and I are so excited to be here. In the room, he watches football while I get ready. And I really go all out, putting on boots, black tights, a jean skirt, and a black Agnes B. top. I feel like I look like a real New Yorker again. When I first moved to Alabama, I would go shopping in Fairhope's quaint little town square, dressed in black, and all the stores were filled with yellows and oranges and pinks, and it seemed like all the women wore bright blush and lipstick, with their hair tucked back in a bow or looking like it just came out of hot rollers. I wanted to yell out, "I'm from New York," but then I'd remember that I'm not, that I'm from that other state in the South that begins with an *A*.

Carrollton Station is only a few minutes away, and we find it with no problem because I have directions that I printed out from the Internet. The bar is small, and I tell the guy at the door that I ordered tickets, and he asks for my credit card, and I see from his list that I'm only one of about ten people who ordered tickets in advance. I start to feel nervous for Brinson, hoping that the place will fill up before he begins.

Mark orders us gin and tonics, and when we walk into the next room, where the stage is, I feel relieved because all of the tables are full and there's a place to sit off to the side, one of those famous church pews, and we sit close together and hold hands next to this pretty, smart-looking girl who's studying a thick book, what I'm sure is a con-law book. Only a first-year would be studying at a bar where live music is about to begin.

Mark starts talking to her, asking her if she's a law student, and she is, of course, a first-year at Tulane, and her name is Jenna. I tell Jenna about how I used to be a lawyer, and she's impressed that I went to NYU, but more impressed that I know Brinson Carr. We start talking about all the songs we like, and she seems to know as much about his music as I do.

"I'll introduce you to him," I tell her, and she nearly falls apart, saying, "I don't know what I'd say. I might just freeze."

Because we were talking, I didn't notice that Brinson was already onstage. He doesn't have a band or anything. It's just him and a couple of guitars and his great-grandfather's banjo.

He starts with a slow one, "Western Sky," and Jenna recognizes it before I do, and she puts away her con-law book and finishes her beer. Mark and I have another round of gin and tonics, and we even order Jenna a beer, and we're all smiling and happy, enjoying the music, and I keep wondering if Brinson has noticed me.

Mark surprises me when he yells out, "Play 'Responsible!'" and Brinson does, and then for Jenna he yells out, "Play 'Seventies Girl!'" and she seems beside herself.

After the show, Brinson sees me and comes back to our table, and we're all kind of drunk, and I'm starting to feel emotional, and I hug Brinson, and he kisses me on the cheek.

"Chandler," he says, "what are you doing here?"

"I'm married and live around here now," I say. "This is my husband, Mark."

Brinson smiles and shakes Mark's hand.

"And this is my friend Jenna," I say. "She's a law student at *Tulane* and *loves* your music."

Brinson gives me a smile like he knows I'm trying to fix him up, wanting him to date yet another friend of mine. "How's Sarah?" he says.

I tell him she's well, acting and singing, and we talk about other friends we have in common from Lakeside Lounge. Then he loses his smile, folds his arms, and tells me about a show he did at the Knitting Factory, which is just blocks from Ground Zero, a few days after September 11. "I didn't think anyone would come," he says. "You had to call ahead to get your name on a list, show your ID to police to get through, and I didn't think anyone would come. But they did. And I donated the money I made."

"That's great," I say.

"It was only about four-hundred bucks."

I nod and smile, and I feel such admiration for Brinson, for still singing, touring around the country, being an artist, helping people in New York, helping me when my father died, and I'm sure, in ways I don't know, helping Jenna.

• • •

Sarah

Instead of getting a cab, I decide to walk down to the Lakeside. It's cold tonight, and I feel a little anxious about the show, but I think the walk will do me good. I'm dressed in black leather pants and a silver low-cut top, and I've got pink glitter on my chest and shoulders. And I have on my new jaguar coat (fake, of course) that I bought on the street. And I just colored my hair black, wearing it in two low ponytails. I feel good about how I look.

I'm on Third Avenue at Tenth Street about to cross over, and on the other side of Third, through the traffic, I think I see Savion Glover walking uptown. He's got on a wool cap, and his dreadlocks are much longer than I remember, but I'm pretty sure it's him.

"Savion!" I yell, over horns honking, motors humming. "Savion!" I yell louder, and he stops and holds his hand to his ear like he's trying to listen, and he sees me because he's smiling now. But traffic is zooming by, and I lose him for a moment, then I see he's beginning to walk uptown again. "You saved my friend!" I yell. "Thank you!" Finally I'm able to run across the street, and I see him a block ahead, and I think about running after him, but I just stand there and watch him until he is lost in the crowd.

I feel dazed and disappointed in myself for missing the opportunity to do something for Chandler, though without realizing it, I'm walking faster toward the Lakeside, swinging my arms, wanting to make the walk sign for the next block, to hurry and get there and be onstage singing and dancing and doing my private-moment exercise, which makes it possible for me not to feel awkward onstage, imagining that I'm dancing at home, alone in front of the mirror, with only Clover watching.

I make the walk sign, and I start moving even faster, trying to make the next one, but then I have to stop because my hand locks into the hand of a man passing me. I look up as he looks up, and he's around my age, with blond hair and glasses, in a suit. He must be coming home from a late night at work, focused like me on something else, and for a moment I wonder if we will let go. Then we do and walk on.

ACKNOWLEDGMENTS

I am especially indebted to the following:

Michelle Tessler at Carlisle & Co., who has been a dream agent, for her guidance and faith and lightning efficiency.

Amanda Patten, my wonderful editor, for her insights and care, for her contagious enthusiasm, and for saying the first time I spoke to her, "I don't mean to *freak* you out, but I *love* your book!"

Elizabeth Bevilacqua, Chris Lloreda, and all the other nice people at Touchstone/Simon & Schuster who have helped along the way.

Clare Conville, for representing my book in the UK, and Harriet Evans, my editor at Michael Joseph/Penguin, both of whom I'm honored to be working with.

Tory Dee Freeman Richman, for her Deborah Harry–like cab hailing, for her Lucky T-shirt, for her hats, and for her glitter. I do not know what I would have done without you.

Lauren Rosolen *(Grazie!)*, Kara Keeley, and Sharbari Ahmed, for their friendship and for reading and rereading.

Patrick Snodgrass, my old college friend, who, unlike the Patrick in the book, never seems to go away.

Sonny Brewer, for his magic touch and for being the first to publish my work in book form.

Paul Giuffre, for literary support, for being from Brooklyn, and for more than I can say.

Rita and Sid Davis, for their appreciation of good books and for making it possible for me to live in New York.

Katy Boulden, the bookstore lady of Fort Smith.

The writing programs at the University of Arkansas (Steve Yates and Jim Whitehead, early encouragers), New York University, and the Sewanee Writers' Conference, and the journal editors who first published my work.

Freedy Johnston, for his music, and for letting Brinson Carr and me borrow his lyrics.

Mom, my first model of a reader and writer, who listened to every chapter over the phone, who oohed and ahhed and laughed and cried, and who caught more than a few errors.

Sidney, for your love, for your confidence in me, for giving me a pretty place in Fairhope, Alabama, so I could focus my life on writing, for teaching me how to be a writer, and for helping with every word.

And Gerri Ellen Christian: I'm sorry I hit you with that golf club.

READING GROUP GUIDE

DISCUSSION POINTS

1. Why do you suppose Jennifer Paddock chose *A Secret Word* as the title of her novel? In what ways do the characters keep secrets from one another, and also from themselves?

2. The novel has an unusual and intriguing structure, split into sixteen chapters that are narrated from three different points of view. Why do you think Paddock chose to tell her story this way? How do the differences between the three young women come through?

3. Do you think the book has a main character, and if so, who is it? Whom did you identify with the most? Which of the secondary characters did you find most interesting? Why?

4. The opening chapter of *A Secret Word* centers on a car accident that takes the life of a boy that all three of the central characters know well. How does this shared tragedy affect their relationships with one another? Do you think it primarily distances them or binds them together?

5. Each chapter is narrated in the first person, and the tone is often very frank and personal, in the manner of a diary entry: "God, it's depressing being me. Old at twenty, Sarah Blair." [p. 29] How does this approach enrich our understanding of the book's characters and themes? How do the three narrators' voices change over time?

6. Chandler and Sarah grow up going to the country club almost daily to play tennis, while Leigh lives with her single mother

who works odd jobs, waiting tables or selling cosmetics. How do their disparate class backgrounds influence their relationships with one another? Later, how do social class and their perceptions of it influence their choices in life?

7. Reflecting on how much she likes Mr. Carey, Chandler's father, Leigh says, "People sometimes ask if I've ever tried to find my father, but I haven't and don't want to. My mother is burden enough." [p. 69] Leigh is not the only one in *A Secret Word* to have a tangled relationship with her parents, and particularly her father. How do the three main characters' feelings about their parents influence their lives? How do you think their choices are affected by their parents' expectations or values?

8. In the chapter called "And When I Should Feel Something," Chandler recounts finding out her father has killed himself, traveling home to Arkansas for the funeral, and then returning to New York City, where she goes again and again to see Savion Glover tap dancing in the Broadway show *Bring in 'Da Noise, Bring in 'Da Funk*. What makes this chapter so compelling and moving? How would you describe the writing style?

9. Near the end of the novel, Chandler recalls a time when she thought Manhattan would save her: ". . . I felt almost happy when I would see the New Yorker hotel sign, and I'd think, *I am home, and I will never leave this place*." [p. 43] Yet she winds up moving back to the South, to Fairhope, Alabama. For her part, Leigh ends up leaving Arkansas to start fresh in Destin, Florida, where she remarks, ". . . I am now certain that I will become who I really am here, to be cured of all that I never was." [p.199] Discuss the significance of place in the lives of the main characters. For example, how does living in New York change Chandler and Sarah? What about them remains the same?

10. When Chandler and Mark Starling are growing closer, he sends her a card with the lyrics to one of her favorite songs, a song she used to listen to after her father died. She describes how the song moved her and made her think about her own

life, even though she couldn't entirely make sense of the words. Are there certain favorite songs of yours that have this kind of effect on you? Do you ever feel that music communicates to you in ways you don't fully grasp?

11. Near the end of the book, Chandler expresses admiration for Brinson Carr, the singer who used to date Sarah, praising him for giving a benefit concert in New York after September 11, for ". . . helping people in New York, helping me when my father died . . ." [p.203] And in the novel's last scene, Sarah sees Savion Glover on the street and yells out to him, "You saved my friend! Thank you!" [p. 203] In what ways do the main characters in *A Secret Word* save one another?

Q&A

1. *If you had to boil it down to its essence, what would you say* A Secret Word *is about?*

It's about many things, equally, I think: friendship, family, love, loss, and surviving loss. What fascinates me most, though, is the thread that runs through all of these things: our connectedness. What I hope will resonate with readers is how we all weave in and out of each other's lives and brush against each other in known ways, of course, but perhaps more often in unknown ways that can be just as influential.

2. *What drew you to themes of family, friendship, and relationships?*

I wanted to write about girls coming into adulthood, and these themes are important for that. Chandler, Sarah, and Leigh eventually leave their families to be on their own, and although the intensity of their friendship with one another appears to fade sometimes, especially between Leigh and the other two, they are connected in a way that will remain essential. Relationships, too, whether they are working or not, are always interesting to write about because they seem very often to sidetrack young women when they're trying to figure out who they want to be and what they want to do in their lives.

3. *When did you start writing, and what inspired you to do so?*

I came to writing relatively late. I was working as a legislative aide on Capitol Hill when I realized that hardly anyone there read fiction. That was a turning point for me, to sit at my desk and feel like a rebel reading Raymond Carver. I moved back home to Arkansas shortly after that and took my first creative writing class, when I was twenty-four. But my whole life I was surrounded by books. When I was growing up, everyone in my family read a lot, especially my mother, who is a writer herself, and for Christmas and birthdays we always gave each other books as presents.

What inspired me about writing from the very beginning was how it helped me make sense of myself and those around me, and what followed was a compulsion to write, which reminded me of how tennis made me feel, when I would concentrate, if not meditate, and get into a rhythm, with the ball, the racquet, the ground, with the whole atmosphere of the court.

4. *A Secret Word has three rather different first-person narrators and spans fifteen years in their lives. What made you decide on this structure for the story? What were the challenges of writing from alternating points of view?*

I decided it would be best to structure the book in alternating voices because I wanted to show the connectedness of the lives, and the families, of three people—slowing down to develop pivotal moments, then speeding past the trivial times that we can all suffer, year after year. So I thought it would be effective if each chapter, at least up until the end, could stand on its own as a viable story, with an arc of development for its particular point-of-view character, while also contributing to the overall progression of the novel.

Managing three distinct voices, which all mature by degree, was a definite challenge for me. Another challenge was trying to have each narrator, at times, give insight into the lives of the other narrators. I don't believe one person can ever really know enough of a story to tell it truthfully or completely anyway. Knowing the truth, or the secrets, about someone, much less about several people, requires multiple perspectives, if not also the breadth of time.

5. *Like Chandler, Leigh, and Sarah, you were raised in Fort Smith, Arkansas. What role does your Southern background play in your writing?*

It plays a significant role, though it might not be as apparent, since my writing doesn't have the rustic atmosphere that you typically see in a Southern novel, but you will find other aspects common to Southern literature, such as a powerful sense of place, an emphasis on family, and a colloquial writing style that I guess could be related to the oral storytelling tradition.

6. *New York City is another principal setting in* A Secret Word. *Compare writing about New York to writing about Arkansas. What were the challenges and rewards of each?*

Because I was living in Fairhope, Alabama, when writing much of this book, they were both equally difficult. I found myself going to Yahoo Maps a lot in order to get the streets right. The reward of writing about Arkansas was that I got to rediscover it. I spent so much of my youth wanting to get out of my hometown, but by writing about it, I realized it was actually quite a wonderful place to grow up. The reward of writing about New York was that I was longing for it and got to live there in my imagination.

7. *How much of a role does autobiography play in your fiction?*

Somewhat of a role. Though many of the characters and situations in *A Secret Word* came strictly from my imagination, I did draw from my own experiences. Like Chandler, I played junior tennis, my father committed suicide, and I married a writer in Sewanee, Tennessee. Like Sarah, I have half-brothers and a half-sister, and I played college tennis and quit. And like Leigh, I worked in a dry cleaners, and sometimes I just feel a lot like Leigh.

8. *What writers and books inspired you when you were growing up? Are there other writers whom you particularly admire and feel have influenced your work?*

I remember as a kid loving *Where the Sidewalk Ends, Charlotte's Web, Where the Red Fern Grows,* then as I got a little older, *To Kill a Mockingbird.* And though there are many writers whom I admire, I'd have to say that the ones who have had the biggest influence on my work are J. D. Salinger, Raymond Carver, Susan Minot, and Jay McInerney. For example, in the beginning, when I was trying to capture the manic rhythms of Sarah's voice, I went to Jay McInerney's *Story of My Life.*

9. *A Secret Word is studded with references to plays, books, poetry, and music. Why did you choose to make the arts so important in the lives of the characters?*

Well, because the arts are so important to me. I know that art is what helped me survive my father's suicide. I feel, in a way, it did save me. For solace, I turned to all the wonderful art New York City offered, like Savion Glover at the Ambassador Theater and Freedy Johnston at Lakeside Lounge, much ·in the same way someone might turn to the church.

10. *What can readers look forward to seeing from you in the future?*

I'm working on a novel set in New York City about the friendship between two women, one from Alabama who is newly married and one from New Jersey who is single, and how that friendship changes because of the marriage. Of course, it will be about other things, too—family, memory, loss, and I'm hoping for a bit of mystery as well.